Books by Albert Marrin

⦿⦿⦿

AZTECS AND SPANIARDS

ycq̃tla ti tetzavitl
yn mal ques.

AZTECS AND SPANIARDS

Cortes and the
Conquest of Mexico

by ALBERT MARRIN

ATHENEUM ⊙ 1986 ⊙ NEW YORK

Library of Congress Cataloging-in-Publication Data

Marrin, Albert   Aztecs and Spaniards.

Bibliography: p. 206.
Includes index.
SUMMARY: Describes the history and culture of the Aztec Indians
in the Valley of Mexico and discusses how the arrival of the
conquistador Hernando Cortes brought about the fall
of their mighty empire.
   I. Mexico—History—Conquest, 1519-1940—Juvenile literature.
2. Cortés, Hernán, 1485-1547—Juvenile literature.
3. Aztecs—History—Juvenile literature.
4. Indians of Mexico—History—Juvenile literature.
[1. Aztecs—History. 2. Indians of Mexico—History. 3. Mexico—
History—Conquest, 1519-1540. 4. Cortes, Hernando, 1485-1547] I. Title.
F1230.M39   1986   972'.01   85-28782
ISBN 0-689-31176-1

Our walls are keening,
Our tears fall down like rain.
Weep, weep, our people,
For we have lost Mexico.

—Aztec poem written about 1523

Contents

AZTECS AND SPANIARDS

1 The City in the Lake

The Valley of Mexico. The year was 1325, the month and day, unknown.

The long, grim years of wandering were finally nearing an end. The people still didn't know their destination, or when they'd reach it, or what it would be like. All they knew was that their god had promised them a homeland—someplace.

They called this god Huitzilopochtli (Weet-zeel-o-po'-tch-tly),* "Hummingbird Wizard" or "Blue Hummingbird of the South." Yet he was nothing like the dainty creature that darts among the blossoms, sipping sweet nectar. Huitzilopochtli was a fierce god, a terrifying god, lord of the sun, war, and hunting. He showed himself always in a blaze of light amid the din of battle.

Wherever Huitzilopochtli's people went, priests led the way carrying his stone idol on a lavishly decorated litter. When the tribe made camp and slept after an exhausting day's march, the god would visit his favorite

---

* Pronunciations of Aztec words are given once in parentheses in the text and again in the index.

3

priests in their dreams. He'd tell them where to go, what to do, and how to do it. He once told them to look for a certain sign, for when it appeared the people must cease their wanderings. They'd be home.

On this day the priests took a trail to the shore of an enormous lake. The sun shone brilliantly. Heatwaves rose from the sandy beach, making the air shimmer. Rays of light danced across the blue water. A gentle breeze raised long, low swells.

In the distance lay two barren islands, hardly more than rock outcroppings surrounded by mudflats fringed with reeds and cattails. The people, who went in constant fear of enemies, built rafts and poled out to the islands, hoping to find a safe place to rest. As the story goes, they splashed ashore on the larger island and noticed a rock with a prickly pear cactus growing out of a crack. A majestic golden eagle perched on the cactus, its talons gripping the plant, its wings beating to give it balance. A rattlesnake, its back broken, hung limp in the bird's hooked beak. It was the sign from their god.

❧   ❧   ❧

These wanderers, whom we know as the Aztecs, were latecomers to the valley. About thirty thousand years ago their ancestors, or people very much like them, arrived in the Americas from Asia. That was the time of the Ice Age and large portions of the earth's surface were covered by glaciers, slow-moving rivers of ice that crushed everything in their path.

With so much of the planet's water locked up as ice, some of the higher portions of the ocean bottoms became exposed as dry land. A land bridge several hundred miles wide spanned the Bering Strait between Siberia and Alaska.

During thousands of years, small bands of hunters muffled in furs moved southward from the windblown

Huitzilopochtli, God of the Sun, War, and Hunting, was the supreme god of the Aztecs. He appears almost tame in this small statue, compared to the descriptions of his great idol, destroyed by the Spaniards.

plains of Siberia in search of game. These earliest American Indians were the true discoverers of the New World, until then uninhabited by humans. Not much taller than five feet, they had high cheekbones, almond-shaped eyes and coarse straight hair of the blackest black. Reddish-brown skin easily absorbed the sun's rays, enabling them to withstand the piercing cold.

As the centuries rolled by, Indian bands moved steadily southward and eastward, penetrating every corner of their new world. In family groups of perhaps twenty to fifty members, they explored from the frozen Arctic and bleak tundra to the southern tip of South America. They made their way into fragrant pine forests and deserts choking with heat and blinding sandstorms. They climbed the towering Andes and paddled canoes to the islands of the Caribbean. During this time, a warming of the earth caused the glaciers to melt, submerging the Bering Strait land bridge beneath the Pacific Ocean once again. Like it or not, they had become Americans forever.

These Indian pioneers lived on whatever nature put before them. They gathered nuts and berries, seeds and fruits. Unpolluted streams and coastal waters teemed with fish and shellfish. Snakes were eaten, along with different kinds of insects. Depending upon where they happened to be, Indians hunted bear, bison, deer, rabbits and birds, especially the wild turkey.

They hunted on foot, because the horse was unknown in the New World until introduced by the Spaniards. Weapons and tools were made of bone, fire-hardened wood, and stone chipped to a point or filed to an edge. Hunting was for the strong and brave. Weaklings died early, killed by the larger animals or driven away by their own people because they couldn't contribute to the common food supply. Still, when game was scarce, even the best hunters suffered. In order to have enough food to go around, the elderly were abandoned and babies killed. If these drastic measures failed, everyone starved and the band disappeared. It was a hard life in which few survived beyond the age of thirty.

About eight thousand years ago, some peoples found a better way of feeding themselves. They learned, perhaps accidentally, that plants could be grown from seeds poked into the ground with a pointed stick. At last, instead of killing or gathering whatever came their way, they were able to produce food for themselves.

By 6000 B.C. farmers in the Americas were growing squash, beans, and chili peppers. Maize, or Indian corn, grew so abundantly and was so nourishing that it became

Aztec agriculture. The man at the left is using a digging stick to make a hole in the earth, into which he drops corn kernels. The people at the right are harvesting the heads of corn. Indian corn, or maize, was the basic food of the farming peoples of the New World. These pictures are from Bernardino de Sahagun's Codex Florentino. A "codex" is a bound book containing sheets of handwritten manuscript. Thus, the Codex Florentino is Sahagun's original manuscript; it is in Florence, Italy.

the basic food of all agricultural peoples. Cotton was also cultivated and woven into cloth, lighter and easier to clean than bug-infested animal skins.

Farming enabled people to abandon the wandering way of life. Since crops had to be carefully tended, permanent settlements grew up around the fields. Population increased, for with a larger and more regular food supply, it was no longer necessary to drive away the old and kill the young. Slowly, isolated farming families formed clans, groups of related families, which in turn united into tribes.

Several of these tribes took up farming in Mexico, a rugged country shaped like a large, curving horn with its wider end opening to the north. Mexico's backbone is made up of branching mountain ranges that follow the coasts along the Pacific Ocean and Gulf of Mexico. The flat coastal areas, receiving twice the rainfall of the mountains, are covered with swamps and jungle. The ancients called them the "Hot Lands" and marveled at their riches: chocolate, rubber, incense, jade. Since jade is a green mineral, and since green is the color of growing things, the Indians valued it more than gold. Here also is found the quetzel bird, whose gold-green feathers rival the sun's brilliance and were sacred.

The Mexican highlands, on the other hand, are a vast plateau, or tableland, broken by the mountains into valleys, each separated from the others. The largest of these is the Valley of Mexico. Lying seven thousand feet above sea level, the Valley of Mexico is ringed by the Sierra, a mountain chain resembling the teeth of a saw. To the south are the twin volcanoes Popocatepetl (Po-po-ka-te'pet-l), "The Smoking Mountain," and his mate, Iztaccihuatl (Es-tak-se-wat'l), "The White Lady," both capped with permanent snow. The mountain air is cool, even in summer. The sky is blue and clear, except during the rainy season, when clouds hug the mountaintops.

Popocatepetl, a 17,887-foot volcano, was known as the "Smoking Mountain" to the Aztecs. It is one of a number of active volcanoes that can be found in Mexico today.

At various times during the twenty-five centuries between 1300 B.C. and 1200 A.D., Mexican tribes built the first civilizations in the Americas. The Olmec lived along the southern Gulf coast, while the Zapotecs cultivated rich lands on the other side of the mountains, along the Pacific. The Maya made their way into Yucatan, a peninsula that juts like a thumb into the Caribbean, pointing toward Cuba. The people of Teotihuacan (Tay-o-tee-wah-ca'n) and the Toltecs prospered in the Valley of Mexico.

Although their languages and customs differed, these people had things in common, either borrowed from each other or developed independently out of similar needs. All were skilled craftsmen: weavers, potters, jewelers, sculptors, featherworkers. All had a system of writing on paper made from the inner bark of the fig tree. Instead of forming words from letters, they expressed ideas with pictures and symbols called "glyphs." They also had a system of mathematics based upon twenty in which every number had a different symbol. Thus:

.1 was a dot or a finger ● *or* Ṗ

10 was shown by ten dots or fingers ⋯⋯ *or* ᏢᏢᏢᏢᏢ ᏢᏢᏢᏢᏢ

20 was represented by a flag Ṗ

400, or 20 times 20, was a feather

410 was a feather and ten dots ⋯⋯

450 was a feather, two flags, and ten dots

8000, or 400 times 20, was a bundle or bag

Although useful for showing fixed quantities like: (three warriors' costumes), their mathematics was useless for the basic operations of addition, subtraction, multiplication, and division. It is impossible, after all, to multiply four feathers by a flag and subtract a finger.

One of the Mexican Indians' greatest achievements was a system of reckoning time—the calendar—without which farmers cannot survive. Everywhere the seasons change, and with them the farmers' chances for a good crop. An early shower might cause them to plant before the growing season, only to see their precious seeds sprout and then wither to dust. It is for this reason that farming peoples have always studied the heavens. For the stars are fixed, immovable, enabling them to tell the seasons by measuring the earth's movements against known points. The Mexican Indians invented a calendar in which each year had eighteen twenty-day months, or 360 days; five "useless" days were left over at the end, during which everyone prayed that the world would go on for another year. Their calendar was more accurate than any known in the Old World until the twentieth century.

The Mexican Indians, and later the Incas of Peru, built cities with romantic-sounding names like Palenque, Chichen Itza, and Monte Alban. But the greatest city was Teotihuacan, which covered over eight square miles and may have had a population of two hundred thousand. Nothing in Mexico can rival its 216-foot-high Temple of the Sun. Teotihuacan was known throughout Mexico and Central America as the "City of the Gods." That name gives us a clue about the purpose of all ancient Mexican cities. Although people built them and lived in them, they were really not meant for humans. They were homes of the gods, centers of prayer, ritual, and sacrifice.

City-builders shared a fear of nature. Farming, despite

its benefits, is a risky business. Too much rain washes crops away, too little withers them in the ground. Hailstones knock tender shoots to pieces. Volcanoes erupt, darkening the sky with grit and burying fields under lava flows. Earthquakes swallow entire villages.

The ancient Mexicans didn't have our ideas of cause and effect. We see natural disasters as the result of laws operating independently of human wishes. Blizzards, we believe, happen because of certain temperature and humidity conditions in the atmosphere, not because snow *wants* to harm us. Indians, however, "took things personally." If something went wrong, it was because the gods, or the powers of nature, decided to make trouble for them.

Indians used their own behavior to understand the actions of the gods. People, they knew, could be loving and cruel, generous and jealous, forgiving and angry. So could the gods. You influence a powerful person with praise and good deeds, begging and bribery. It was the same with the gods. We call this "anthropomorphism," the giving of human qualities to anything that is not human.

The cities of ancient Mexico existed to serve the gods so that they'd favor the people. Without their favor, the crops would die and the people vanish from the face of the earth. Priests, specially trained men and women, served the gods, prayed for their kindness, and led the community in songs and dances in their honor. Only the most valuable and beautiful things were worthy as gifts for the gods: food, flowers, jewels. And life itself. Priests sacrificed butterflies, birds, and animals to win the gods' favor. Sometimes they sacrificed other people. All the Mexican city-builders practised human sacrifice to a greater or lesser extent. Individuals, they believed, had to die so that the gods might be pleased and so that the whole of the people might live.

The city-builders had one other thing in common: their civilizations eventually collapsed. For no matter how hard the priests tried, they really couldn't control nature. Crops failed. Insect pests swarmed. The soil lost its fertility. Fierce barbarians swooped down from the north. These Chichimecs, "Dog People," wore animal skins, ate raw meat, and had a deadly new weapon: the bow and arrow. They couldn't read, but they could fight, and they slaughtered the farmers. People abandoned the cities, leaving them deserted, lonely, open to the ravages of time and weather. They stand today, empty shells, for tourists to visit and admire—and wonder about.

When the Toltecs' capital of Tula in the Valley of Mexico was destroyed about 1200 A.D., the survivors scattered across the valley. Toltecs and Chichimecs, who learned to farm from them, settled along the shores of an enormous lake. The Lake of the Moon covered four hundred square miles, but was only nine to twelve feet deep. At night its calm surface acted as a mirror, reflecting the moon's silvery disk.

The Lake of the Moon was divided into five sections, each with its own name, although they formed part of the same body of water. Three northern sections—Texcoco, Xaltocan, Zumpango—were salty, owing to minerals that washed down from the mountains. The two southern sections—Chalco and Xochimilco—were fed by melting snow and remained fresh.

The early arrivals took the best lakeside lands for themselves and built new cities like Texcoco, Chalco, Culhuacan, Tacuba and Xochimilco, "Fields of Flowers." Citizens of these cities never saw themselves as one people with a common heritage and destiny. Each city was actually a tiny nation that regarded its neighbors with suspicion and hostility. Neighbors, if weak, were attacked and their lands seized. Strong neighbors were given sweet words and tribute, "protection money," in order to be left alone. War and bullying were as normal as sunrise and sunset in the Valley of Mexico.

The Aztecs were the last people to arrive in the valley. Their origins and earliest history are a mystery and are likely to remain so forever. All that is known for certain is that they spoke the Nahuatl language, "the pleasant sound," and came from Aztlan, or Place of the Herons, in northern Mexico. No one today knows the location of Aztlan; the Aztecs—People of Aztlan—forgot its location during their wanderings.

Legend says that in the year 1168 Teoyaotlatohue-huitzilopochtli, "The Divine Lord of War, Great Huitzilo-pochtli," commanded the Aztecs to move south in search of a better homeland. They were to advance cautiously, sending pioneers ahead to plant crops wherever the land seemed fertile. When the crop was ready, the tribe moved up to harvest it while the pioneers went forward once again. Wherever the Aztecs went, they carried the idol of Hummingbird Wizard and "fed" it with the hearts and blood of warriors taken in battle.

Legend ends and history begins when the Aztecs arrived in the Valley of Mexico. They were not welcomed, there being no room for strangers in a land already over-crowded. City dwellers, moreover, despised them for their coarse, brutal ways. Their wandering life had welded them into a tight community united against the world. Kindly toward one another, they were as tough and hard toward outsiders as the stone of Huitzilopochtli's idol.

Yet that toughness made them useful. They were allowed to settle for a few years at a time in the territories they passed through, provided they fought for the local rulers. During one stopover, they were given a campsite on a rocky hillside crawling with rattlesnakes. The official sent by the ruler to check up on them reported that they

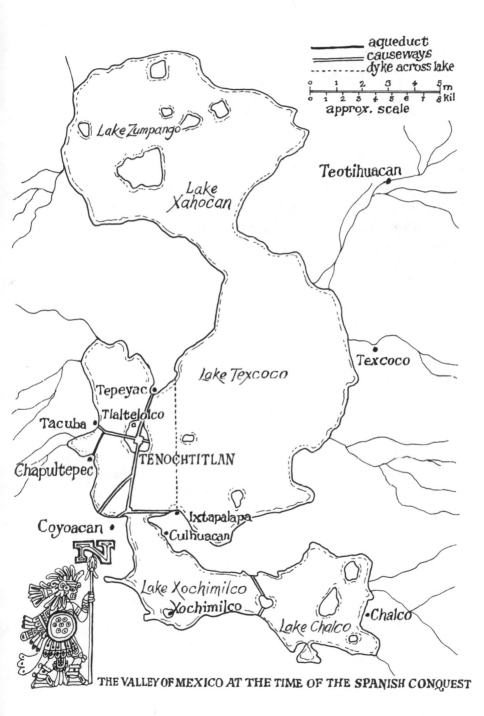

aqueduct
causeways
dyke across lake

approx. scale

Lake Zumpango

Lake Xahocan

Teotihuacan

Lake Texcoco

Texcoco

Tepeyac

Tlaltelolco

Tacuba

Chapultepec

TENOCHTITLAN

Coyoacan

Ixtapalapa

Culhuacan

Lake Xochimilco

Xochimilco

Lake Chalco

Chalco

THE VALLEY OF MEXICO AT THE TIME OF THE SPANISH CONQUEST

were cheerful and content. Not a rattlesnake was to be seen, since they'd eaten them all. The Aztecs were evicted when they lost their usefulness or their employers became frightened of them. There was plenty to fear, since the Aztecs raided nearby villages for sacrificial victims and kidnapped women, whom they'd marry and adopt into the tribe.

They had foolishly sacrificed the daughter of the lord of Culhuacan (Cool-wah-ca'n) and were fleeing his soldiers when Hummingbird Wizard guided them to the islands in the lake. Before tending to their own needs, they built him a temple of reeds on the spot where the eagle had perched on the cactus. Cottages of the same material sheltered the people during the years of struggle that followed.

The Aztecs gave their settlement—it could hardly be called a city—the double name Mexico-Tenochtitlan (Ten-otch-ti-tlan). Mexico means "The Town in the Middle of the Lake of the Moon." Tenochtitlan is "The Place of the Prickly Pear Cactus." Both names were used together or separately, although Tenochtitlan seems to have been preferred. The Aztecs often called themselves *Mexica* or *Tenochca* after their homeland. The glyph of Tenochtitlan was an eagle eating a snake, the same symbol shown on the flag of the Republic of Mexico today.

The islands may not have been beautiful or comfortable, but they had certain advantages. Their location, three miles from the shore at the nearest point, made them easy to defend. The soil, what little there was of it, was extremely fertile. The first maize crops were bountiful.

The lake itself yielded rich harvests of birds, fish, and freshwater shrimps. A living film covered the water near shore; jellylike strings of insect eggs and the larvae of water flies could be skimmed from the surface and eaten raw. Frogs were a delicacy, as were tadpoles and young salamanders. Aztec cooks minced these creatures with peppers and stuffed them into cornmeal envelopes called *tamales*.

The Aztecs prospered in their island home. Hundreds, then thousands, of canoes set out for the mainland each day loaded with trade goods. Each night they returned with loads of turkeys and small hairless dogs for their cooking pots; these dogs, which couldn't bark, were raised on special farms as we raise poultry. Heavy loads of timber and stone had to be hauled across the lake on rafts. The people were determined that Huitzilopochtli should have the most glorious temple on earth, one that would last forever.

Since their islands were small, the Aztecs enlarged them whenever necessary. They began by weaving reed baskets eight feet wide by fifty feet long. The baskets were anchored in the shallows and filled with rich mud scooped from the lake bottom. Fast-growing willow trees were planted and, in time, their roots poked through the basket-work, anchoring the baskets permanently. Each new crop was planted in a fresh layer of mud until the farmer had a rectangular strip of solid land called a *chinampa*. Lines of *chinampas* were arranged opposite each other, forming between them a grillwork of canals around the original islands. Each farm family built its cottage on its own *chinampa* alongside a canal. The only way to reach most places in Tenochtitlan was by canoe. If the rulers decided more land was needed, they simply had the canal filled in with mud and stone.

Although safe in their island home, the Aztecs never lost their aggressiveness; if anything, operating from a secure base made them more aggressive. As they became familiar with the lakeside cities, they formed alliances to further their interests. We should remember always, as they did, that Tenochtitlan had no friends, only allies. Its people had contempt for outsiders, and the outsiders saw them as people it was useful to have on their side.

At first Tenochtitlan was allied with the cities of Texcoco and Tacuba. Together they made war on others, seizing land and slaves and demanding tribute: jade, cloaks of finely woven quetzel feathers, cotton cloth, gold, jewelry, food.

The Aztecs, however, gained influence with each passing generation, until Tenochtitlan dominated the alliance. Its Chief Speakers, or rulers, were shrewd men skilled at gaining power and using others for their own purposes. The early Chief Speakers had such fierce names as Smoking Shield, Angry Lord Who Shoots the Sky, The Whip, Leg of Chalk, and Water Monster. Under them, the Aztecs became so strong that they alone decided when the alliance waged war; they even began to appoint rulers for their allies. Such high-handedness was resented, but the Aztecs shut their ears to protests. Tenochtitlan, its rulers believed, was too powerful to have to listen to complaints about injustice.

In less than two centuries the Aztecs rose from barbarian wanderers to become lords of a vast empire. By 1519, the year the Spaniards arrived, they controlled eighty thousand square miles of territory extending from the Gulf of Mexico to the Pacific, from the green hills of Oaxaca (Wah-ha'h-cah) in the south to the brown wastelands of the north. The empire included fifteen million people, mostly non-Aztecs, and received tribute from 489 communities. Not even Teotihuacan at the height of its power could boast of such an empire.

～   ～   ～

The Aztec capital grew along with its power. Its population expanded from a few hundred fugitives to at least three hundred thousand citizens. No city in the Americas could match it in 1519; indeed, it was larger by far than any European capital at the time, including London, Paris, Rome, and Madrid.

Having defeated the lakeside cities, the Chief Speakers felt secure enough to link Tenochtitlan permanently to the mainland. They ordered the people to build three causeways, long, straight highways of stone pierced in many places and the openings spanned by bridges. These were not only for convenience but safety. Even if an invading army managed to come over the causeways, it would find itself imprisoned in the city once the bridges were cut.

The causeways, surrounded by water on either side, became streets when they reached Tenochtitlan. The streets were paved with chunks of stone pounded into the earth to form a hard surface. Even so, water was everywhere, as most streets ran alongside the canal between two *chinampas*, which were in turn linked by scores of bridges. Strollers on land were able to keep up conversations with friends as they paddled to their destination.

Tenochtitlan became more magnificent as one followed the causeways to their end in the central square. The city's outskirts were crowded with farmers' cottages made of straw and mud. Each cottage had one tiny room with an earthen floor, a low open doorway, and no windows or chimney to let out the cooking fires' smoke. Household goods were few and simple: straw brooms and baskets, clay jars and wooden digging sticks, for the plow was unknown in old Mexico. Wooden chests held the family's valuables. There were no chairs or beds; the farmers used straw mats for sitting and sleeping. Tortillas, a kind of flat bread of cornmeal and the Aztecs' basic food, were prepared on a flat stone hearth heated red-hot with twigs and chips of wood.

Once inside the city, the houses became grander. The houses of skilled craftsmen and merchants were made of

Aerial view of Tenochtitlan as imagined by a modern artist. The city of some three hundred thousand was built on an island in the middle of the Lake of the Moon. Causeways, the longest of which is in the foreground, were built of stone to link the island to the mainland. Cortes came over this causeway with his army in 1519. Then, as now, Mexico City was surrounded by mountains, which stand out clearly in the distance.

adobe, sunbaked clay bricks. These one-story buildings
had four or five rooms arranged around a courtyard that
provided shade and space for a garden; the Aztecs loved
flowers and decorated Tenochtitlan with colorful blossoms
from end to end. Like the farmers' homes, the furniture in
these houses was simple, only of better quality. The wealthy
had wooden chairs, but even the Chief Speaker slept on a

straw mat spread on the floor for the night and rolled up in the morning.

The wealthiest people, government officials and the most prosperous merchants, lived nearest the city's center. Their houses, also of one story, were made of whitewashed stone or painted with reddish clay.

Everything about Tenochtitlan sparkled with cleanliness. When the city outgrew its freshwater springs, it began a vast engineering project to bring water from the mainland. An aqueduct was run across the lake from the springs at Chapultepec (Cha-po'ol-tepec), "Hill of the Grasshopper," a distance of nearly four miles. The engineers left nothing to chance. The aqueduct, built of stone and mortar, had two channels, each as wide as a man's body. Only one channel was used at a time, allowing the water to be switched into the other when the first channel had to be cleaned. The aqueduct passed through hollow bridges built over the canals. To get drinking water, a family member parked his canoe under a water-bridge and handed up his jars, which a water-drawer filled at a small cost.

All Aztecs, even the poorest, bathed once a day in the lake or in a small, igloo-shaped sweatlodge attached to each house. The bather built a fire against the outer wall, then crawled inside through a narrow opening. He or she sat on the ground and sprinkled the wall, by now glowing with heat, with water, raising clouds of steam. Using the roots of a plant that produced a soapy lather, the bather rubbed down arms, legs and chest, vigorously striking the back with bunches of long grass to shake the dirt loose. Few, if any, Europeans at this time bathed as often or stayed as clean. Powerful kings merely spattered themselves with perfume to hide their foul body odors. A queen of Sweden in the 1500's was proud of her black hands, boasting that she never washed them.

Tenochtitlan itself was cleaner than any European city, where filth was tossed into the unpaved streets to mix with the mud. A thousand men swept and washed Tenochtitlan's streets every day. Garbage was collected and buried in the marshes at the city's edge. Public toilets were located at regular intervals along the streets and causeways. Human wastes were saved and put to good use as fertilizer in the fields. The pure mountain air, plus the cleanliness of the people, saved Tenochtitlan from the epidemics that regularly ravaged European cities.

The causeways ended at Tenochtitlan's main square, a huge space enclosed by the Serpent Wall, a stone wall decorated with paintings of writhing snakes and carvings of snake heads with curved fangs. Fronting the wall, on either side of the square, were government warehouses brimming with tribute and arsenals filled with weapons. Here, too, were the royal palaces, two-story buildings with hundreds of rooms, halls, and gardens.

To walk through one of the three gates in the Serpent Wall was to enter another world. Here was the Aztec holy of holies, the most sacred spot on earth. The area, paved with large white cobblestones polished to a high gloss, was filled with religious statues, monuments, and round calendar stones. Dominating the skyline were the *Teocalli*, the great flat-topped pyramids crowned with the temples of the gods. Every day, without fail, as we shall see, priests sacrificed victims in front of the temples.

North of the central square lay the section of the city known as Tlatelolco (Tla-tel-o'l-co). Built on the smaller of the two islands, Tlatelolco was bound to the main city forever when the narrow waterway between them was filled in. Tlatelolco had its own central square, complete with pyramid and temple. Its open-air market may have been the largest in the world. Sixty thousand people crowded the market daily, buying and selling goods of

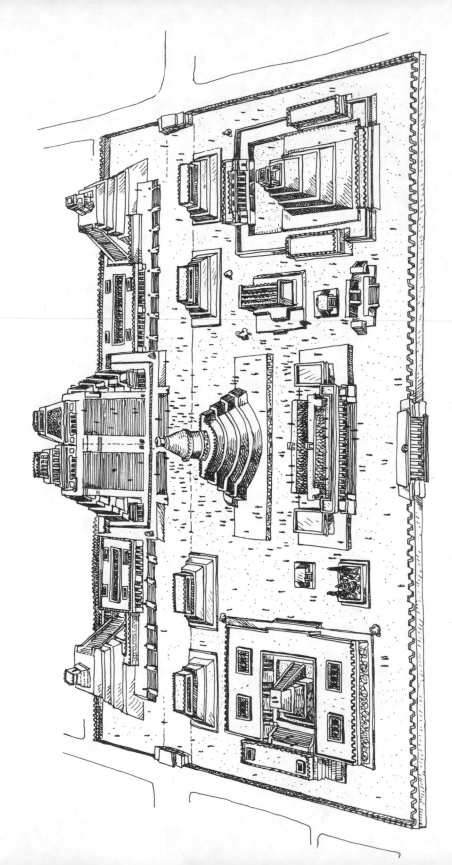

◀ *Aerial view of the sacred precinct of Tenochtitlan. The rounded structure in the center of the picture is the Temple of Quetzelcoatl, Feathered Serpent, God of Wisdom. Across from the temple is the ball court; to its right is the Tzompantli, skull rack, where the heads of sacrificial victims were displayed.*

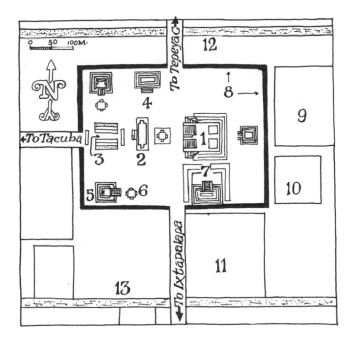

MAIN STRUCTURES IN THE SACRED PRECINCT OF TENOCHTITLAN, 1519

1. Great Temple of Huitzilopochtli and Tlaloc.
2. Tzompantli (skull rack).
3. Court for sacred ball game.
4. Temple of the Snake.
5. Temple of Xipe Totee.
6. Platform for gladiatorial stone.
7. Temple of Tezcatlipoca.
8. Serpent Wall, surrounding the sacred precinct.
9. Palace of Lord Water Monster.
10. Royal Aviary.
11. Palace of Montezuma II.
12, 13. Canals.

every description. Trade was by barter, since the Aztecs didn't use money. Certain items, however, had fixed values and could be used as coins. Feather capes, quills filled with gold dust, and cocoa beans were valuable in themselves and accepted for any purchase.

᪣   ᪣   ᪣

The Aztecs led orderly, disciplined lives free from any of the cares that trouble modern peoples. Everybody from the humblest to the mightiest knew their place in the scheme of things. They knew who they were, where they belonged, and what was expected of them at all times. The idea of the individual's being separate from the community would have struck them as unnatural, inhuman, terrifying. A person's life wasn't his own, but belonged to the tribe, which counted for everything. Without the tribe's nurture and protection, the strongest person could look forward to a life that was nasty, painful, and short.

The tribe was the city, made up in turn by the *calpulli*, the twenty clans, or family groupings. Each clan had its own chief and neighborhood in Tenochtitlan. The chief was assisted by a council of elders elected by the clan's warriors; the Aztecs respected the elderly, believing that people grew wiser with age.

Chief and council controlled the lives of their clan's members. They distributed the land, which belonged not to the farmer who lived and worked on it, but to the community. Education, aid to the poor, and the law courts were also the responsibility of clan officials. Each neighborhood had its own clan temple which, though smaller than those enclosed by the Serpent Wall, was no less sacred.

During the early days of Tenochtitlan, respresentatives of the *calpulli* elected the Chief Speaker from among the best men in the tribe; in later times he was chosen from among the members of the royal family. The ruler was always a man, because the Aztecs believed that women belonged at home, not meddling in the serious business of government. One Aztec proverb said that men preferred wives with both ears plugged and mouths sewn shut.

The Chief Speaker was all-powerful, combining in himself the offices of high priest, commanding general, and supreme judge. Upon being elected, he was reminded by the priests of his duties toward the less fortunate: "Do not forget the poor, dying of hunger, and distribute food to the aged."

The rules the Aztecs lived by were few, simple, and unquestionable. Men were expected to marry at twenty, women at sixteen, for to be unmarried was to remain a child in the eyes of the tribe. Marriage was a serious step, too serious to be left to the young. Family members took charge of the arrangements from start to finish. When a son came of age, his father asked about eligible young women among neighboring clans. It wasn't necessary for a couple to meet before the wedding day, only that their families should agree on the conditions of the marriage.

One day an old woman who acted as a matchmaker visited the girl's parents. She said that she knew of a young man whose father hoped to see him married to such a fine girl. Good manners required the parents to make excuses at first: their daughter was too young, too clumsy, a poor cook, they said. Still, everyone knew how to take these excuses, as the Aztecs liked to do things calmly, without seeming too eager.

When the matchmaker returned a few days later, the families were ready to talk seriously. The father of the would-be bridegroom sent presents to the girl's parents, who in turn said what they'd give as the bride's dowry, the gifts she'd bring to her husband. Now only the wedding date remained to be settled.

A priest was called in and given the couple's birth

dates, which he checked against a sacred calendar to find a lucky wedding day. That day was filled with excitement in both households. Toward noon, the guests arrived at the bride's house with gifts of feather capes, cotton cloth, and other useful things. The guests—relatives, teachers, friends, neighbors, clan officials—sat down to a feast that the women had been preparing for a week. Between courses they gave the couple long lectures on their responsibilities to each other and to the tribe.

At nightfall the wedding party set out for the bridegroom's home. The bride's arms and legs were decorated with red feathers and her face lightly powdered with yellow clay. Her skirt and blouse, embroidered with flower patterns, were as colorful as she. Since it was bad luck to touch the ground between her old and new home, she made the journey on the matchmaker's back. As friends led the way with torches, passersby shared their happiness with songs and cries of "Oh, happy girl!"

Arriving at the groom's home, the couple sat beside one another on two sleeping mats. After some more speeches, the matchmaker tied the corner of the young man's cloak to the tail of his bride's blouse. It was that easy; from the moment she tied the knot, they were husband and wife. We still use the phrase "to tie the knot" when a couple is married.

In time, the wife announced that she was going to be a mother. Her news brought joy to the whole neighborhood. Another feast was held which, if less elaborate than the wedding banquet, was just as happy.

Soon after the child's birth, a priest was called in to help select a lucky name from his sacred books. Boys' names gave a sense of action and of their destiny as warriors. Among these names were Hungry Coyote, Angry Turkey, Speaking Eagle, and Bee in the Reeds. Girls received dainty, feminine names like Jade Doll and Precious

Plume of the Quetzel Bird. Flower names were especially popular: Rain Flower, Turquoise Maize-Flower, Ant Flower.

"Sweet child, my jewel, my precious feather," parents whispered to their newborn. No Aztec child was ever unloved or unwanted, since children were the tribe's future. It was for this reason that love and tenderness were combined with strict discipline. Unless the child became a good citizen, it was useless to the tribe, merely another mouth to feed.

Parents lectured youngsters on their duties and how to get along with others. A good person had to be considerate, generous, truthful, and loyal. "Respect and salute your elders," a father said, "and greet them properly. Console the poor with good deeds and kind words. Honor, love, serve, and obey your parents. Do not follow madmen, who honor neither father nor mother. Do not mock the old, the sick, the crippled, or those in serious trouble, but pray to the gods, and hope the same will not happen to you. Do not dress too strangely, because this is a sign of little intelligence. Do not enter or leave before your elders, nor cross in front of them, nor speak to them first. When you eat, give part of the food to him who comes begging for it. If anything is given to you, no matter how little, do not despise it, or become angry, or think that you deserve more, because you lose character in the sight of the gods and man. Do not be a gambler or a thief. Keep on the straight path, sow and reap, and eat the produce of your own labor. Thus you will live happily and your parents will love you."

The only thing Aztec children were not taught was to think for themselves. They learned early in life that the authorities—parents, teachers, priests, rulers, army officers—must never be questioned or challenged. Obedience, instant, total obedience, was the only way the tribe could keep its unity in a world filled with enemies. Without that unity, the Aztecs knew that they would disappear as a people.

Children helped with the family's work as soon as they could walk. At first the chores were a game, like toddling after father carrying a little stick. But as the child grew, so did the chores. Fathers taught sons their trades, mothers taught daughters how to be housewives.

Aztec parents had no patience with laziness or disobedience. Loving as they were, they could also be harsh and punishing. Boys had their hands and chests pricked with cactus needles until the blood flowed. Or they were tied hand and foot and left outdoors overnight, naked, in a mud puddle.

Girls were supposed to be modest and have nothing to do with boys until marriage. Girls never went out by themselves, but always in the company of a chaperon, an older woman, usually a married relative. When walking in the street, a girl was supposed to keep her head bent, eyes on the ground. If she looked at a boy or worse, spoke to one, she was punished by having her head held over a heap of burning chili peppers and forced to inhale the bitter smoke.

Children quickly learned that discipline in the home was mild compared to the tribe's ideas of law and justice. The Aztecs had a system of courts in which judges were appointed by the Chief Speaker and the *calpulli* chiefs. Judges were men chosen for their honesty and common sense. Aztec law was simple, straightforward, and had no need for trained lawyers. A judge had only to hear a complaint and give his verdict without delay.

The Aztecs had no prisons, nor did they believe in trying to reform evildoers. Those convicted of crimes were dealt with swiftly—and permanently. Punishment depended upon the seriousness of the offense, although all punishments were harsh. People who lied about their

Executing a criminal by strangulation. The Aztecs had few laws, but the laws they had were severe, carrying the death penalty for many offenses. The prickly pear cactus sketched at the upper right is the symbol of Tenochtitlan. (Redrawn from the Codex Florentino.)

neighbors had their lips cut off. Thieves caught in the Tlatelolco market were tied to a post and everyone threw stones at them until they died. Murderers were executed in public by strangulation or having their heads crushed with a heavy stone.

The Aztecs made a powerful liquor called *octli* or *pulque* from the juice of the maguey plant, but they feared alcohol, because drunkards seemed to be taken over by demons who made them forget their duties to the tribe. Anyone seen drunk in public was automatically put to death. Commoners were beaten with clubs or strangled in front of the young men as a lesson; noblemen were drowned in private. Only elderly men and women were allowed to get drunk, especially on happy occasions, because they'd soon be traveling to the spirit world.

Judges and government officials weren't beyond the reach of the law. The Aztecs believed that the more authority a person had, the greater must be their respect for law. A corrupt official was punished especially hard for violating his trust. Accepting bribes, giving false reports, and handing down unjust decisions carried the death penalty. Harsh as it was, Aztec law never allowed torture, common in Europe for gaining information and punishment. The people were shocked at the very idea of causing unnecessary suffering or pain for its own sake.

Besides watching executions, Aztec youngsters became used to seeing slaves auctioned off or going about Tenochtitlan on errands for their masters. Slavery wasn't the same in Mexico as in Europe and, later, the United States. The Aztecs couldn't imagine a person's being born into slavery, much less having to remain a slave for life. They thought of slavery as a misfortune, like illness, that could strike anyone. Slaves were to be pitied for their bad luck, not mocked or mistreated. Losing your freedom didn't make you any less of a human being.

Some slaves were foreigners, such as war prisoners with special skills or part of the tribute of a conquered city. Most, however, came from among the Aztecs themselves. The courts usually condemned to slavery small-time thieves and people unable to pay their debts. Others became slaves voluntarily. During hard times, free citizens might sell themselves into slavery for a few years in return for food to feed their families. A poor farmer sometimes offered a son as a slave in exchange for a loan of food or seed. Slavery carried no shame. Widows often married one of their slaves, and Itzcoatl (Eet'z-co-atl), "Obsidian Snake," one of Tenochtitlan's greatest rulers (1427–1440), was the son of a slave woman.

Aztec slaves, though unfree, had certain basic rights. No matter what they had done, their families remained free; only children of traitors could be born into slavery. Slaves kept their property and could acquire more, including slaves of their own. And the road to freedom always remained open. Slaves could buy back their freedom by returning the value of the goods stolen or by paying their debts. An escaped slave didn't have to pay anything. If he or she ran away from the slave market nobody, on pain of death, could stand in their way. Only the owner or his sons could give chase. They had to be fast, for any slave that ran into the Chief Speaker's palace was automatically free.

Owners had to be careful about how they treated their human property. Killing a slave, or even hurting one, carried the death penalty under Aztec law. Only laziness or disobedience put a slave's life in danger. If a slave was

Slave market scene. Slaves, men, women, and children, were displayed prior to sale with wooden collars around their necks. The collar was thought a necessary precaution, for any slave who escaped into the nearby palace of the Chief Speaker was automatically free. (Picture redrawn from Codex Florentino.)

sold three times and still didn't mend his ways, he was placed in a wooden cage and sold for sacrifice to the gods.

~ ~ ~

Upon reaching the age of seven or eight, Aztec youngsters began their formal education in a public school. The Aztecs were the only people in the world at the time to have free schools that every child had to attend. From this time on, the tribe took charge of the children, shaping them in its own way for its own purposes.

Girls went to schools attached to temples to learn religion and women's crafts of weaving and embroidery. The girls ate and slept at school, living under the watchful eyes of elderly priestesses. Discipline was stricter than at home. The daily routine was built around work and prayer, with no room for childish games and laughter. To teach self-control, the girls were made to sit perfectly still without moving a muscle or saying a word. A girl usually left school to be married or, if she chose, stayed on to become a priestess.

There were two types of boys' school. Sons of ordinary citizens, including slaves, attended the clan school, the *Telpuchcalli* (Tel-pootch-kahl-lee), or "House of Youth." Each temple had a *Calmecac* (Kahl-may-kahk) school, or "Row of Houses," reserved for the sons of the nobility and the wealthiest merchants. Both types of school, however, existed for the same purpose: to prepare youngsters for citizenship. And citizenship meant serving the gods as well as going to war. Religion and war went hand-in-hand, because, to the Aztecs, they were one and the same.

Religion was the most important part of Aztec life. Everything they did, thought about and believed had religious meaning. Prayers begging the gods for favors, or thanking them for favors, were constantly on their lips. When something went wrong, they believed it was because the gods were offended. At such times they tortured themselves by passing knotted strings through slits cut in their tongues. Only pain, they believed, could win the gods' forgiveness.

Like all native Americans, the Aztecs were polytheists; that is, they had many gods. Indeed, they "collected" gods, worshipping not only their own but those of conquered peoples, whose idols were kept in a special temple. They did this not out of respect but practicality: they couldn't take the chance of overlooking a god, forgetting to honor it properly. For the gods were everywhere, all-knowing, all-powerful, and easily offended.

The Aztecs always feared that the gods would turn the forces of nature against them, as they'd done during the previous Four Suns. Legends told of Four Suns, or past ages, when the world was destroyed, only to be recreated by a different god each time. The First Sun ended when jaguars ate up the human race. During the Second Sun,

Self-sacrifice. An Aztec passes sharp reeds through his tongue to draw blood, which will be offered to the gods. Blood was considered sacred, the source of life for both humans and gods. (Picture redrawn from the Codex Telleriano.)

Mask of Tlaloc, God of Rain, is made of mother-of-pearl and turquoise. The god's tongue sticks out to lap up the raindrops. The Aztecs went in for realism in their art, and sometimes masks were made of real human skulls.

hurricanes destroyed the world and people turned into monkeys. The Third and Fourth Suns were brought to a close by a rain of fire and floodwaters that drowned the survivors.

And the Fifth Sun, their present age? Only human sacrifice could save the world and the people in it.

The Aztecs weren't the only believers in human sacrifice. At one time or another it was practiced in Europe, Asia, Africa, the Pacific world, and South America. The early city dwellers of Mexico, as we've seen, also offered their gods human lives. Yet there was a difference. While others sacrificed only occasionally, perhaps a few dozen victims a year, the Aztecs went overboard. Human sacrifice became the core of a bloodstained religion that demanded ever more victims. The Aztecs acted as if their gods could never be satisfied no matter how many died for them.

Depending on their importance and role in nature, different gods required different kinds of sacrifices. Each type of sacrifice had special meaning, and only that type would satisfy a given god.

Huitzilopochtli, the Aztec tribal god, had the grandest shrine within the square enclosed by the Serpent Wall. The whole area was dominated by his two-hundred-foot-high pyramid. A double row of steps led from the ground to the pyramid's top. The steps were so steep that anyone climbing them couldn't see the top; it was like walking straight up into the sky.

Instead of narrowing to a peak, like the pyramids of ancient Egypt, the Aztec pyramid's top was leveled to form a temple platform. Huitzilopochtli shared the platform with Tlaloc (Tla'h-loc), god of rain, whose name means "He Who Makes Things Grow." While Hummingbird Wizard warmed the earth as the sun, his companion watered the crops. Together they made life possible in the Valley of Mexico.

Their temples were built of giant wooden beams that supported high, sloping roofs decorated with the gods' symbols. Tlaloc's temple was painted with vertical blue and white stripes representing rain. Huitzilopochtli's temple was painted with red and white stripes representing blood and bones; stone skulls glistened against the red background. A low block of stone stood in front of each temple. Every day without fail, these stones were bathed in "divine water"—human blood.

The Aztecs had observed that the heart is a strange, wonderful thing. It is a sort of living being inside another living being, the only part of the body that can be heard and felt to move, seeming to have a life of its own. They noticed also that, in dead people, the heart no longer beat and the blood no longer flowed, so they concluded that: blood is life, blood is nourishment that the heart sends coursing through the body. Therefore it seemed logical to them that the gods, so much like humans in other ways, should need blood in order to live.

Blood was especially important to Huitzilopochtli. As the sun god, he fought a never-ending war against Tezcatlipoca (Tes-cat-li-po'-ca), the Smoking Mirror, god of night. Each morning Huitzilopochtli rose brilliantly in the east, full of life, lord of the daytime sky. All day he bathed the earth in his lifegiving light. But in the evening, as he dipped over the western horizon, he began a life-and-death struggle. Smoking Mirror cast a black, velvety shroud across the heavens, studding the darkness with stars, cold, distant specks of light.

Huitzilopochtli had always fought through the darkness to bring the new day. But he might not always be victorious. One night he might falter and grow weak, failing to appear next morning. The result was too awful to think about, for the world would perish. To prevent this tragedy, the Aztecs had to keep the sun strong with a steady

The god Tezcatlipoca, Lord of Darkness, was the enemy of Hummingbird Wizard, the sun god, threatening to swallow him in blackness and put an end to the world. (Picture redrawn from the Codex Borgia.)

diet of human hearts and blood. By giving him the source of human life, they guaranteed his life, and with it the continuation of life on earth.

Victims sacrificed to Huitzilopochtli were usually captives taken in war. Individually or in groups, they were escorted up the hundred and fourteen steps of the Great Pyramid by Aztec warriors. They knew their fate, for they also believed in human sacrifice. Had things gone differently, they'd have sacrificed Aztec prisoners.

They walked in a straight line, one behind the other, heads erect, bodies painted with red and white stripes, saying not a word. Stone snakes guarding the staircase followed their every movement with eyes of colored glass. On a busy day, blood would flow in streams past them down the steps, forming sticky, reddish-brown pools at the pyramid's base.

52.

As priests hold the victim down on the sacrificial stone, the high priest cuts out his heart and offers it to the sun. The knife, which he holds in his left hand, was a leaf-shaped blade of sharpened flint. (Redrawn from the Codex Florentino.)

Each prisoner in turn saw the sacrificial stone at the last moment, when he mounted the top step. Then he saw the priests. Many brave men fainted at the sight.

Sacrificing priests wore long black robes embroidered with pictures of skulls, bones, and curling intestines. Their bodies were also black, smeared with an oily goo made of the burned sap of the rubber tree mixed with crushed spiders, scorpions, and centipedes. They were thin as skeletons from constant fasting. Their hair was never cut and reached to their waists, even to the ankles. It was so caked with blood and matted that it couldn't be separated. The priests' fingernails were long and curved, claw-like, because, like the hair, they were never cut. They took massive doses of Jimson weed and a mushroom known as "Flesh of the Gods." These narcotics could bring brilliant colors and visions of writhing snakes before their eyes. Without drugs, they might not have been able to go through with the sacrifices.

The moment the victim set foot on the topmost step, five priests rushed forward. Quickly, in a single motion, two seized him by either arm, forcing him backward, while two others pulled his legs from under him and flopped him, chest upward, over the bloodstained stone. A fifth priest held his head. Pinned, unable to twist away, he stared at a sixth priest dressed in scarlet robes with red painted body. In his hand he held the sacrificial knife, a foot-long blade of flint sharpened to a razor edge.

The victim's screams—if he still had the voice to scream—were drowned out by the huge snakeskin drum that stood nearby. As the red priest raised the knife, the drum sounded, booming over the city, over the lake, over the valley beyond.

The priest opened the victim's chest, slipped his hand into the wound, and tore the heart from the body. The heart, still throbbing and spraying blood, was held toward the sun, then set aside to be burned in a stone vessel in front of Huitzilopochtli's idol. Sometimes the heart was touched to the idol's lips to "feed" it. Carvings of the god on the temple walls were smeared with blood.

Even in death the victim had his uses. The corpse was rolled down the pyramid steps to other priests waiting below. They removed the head and set it on the nearby *tzompantli* (tsom-pan-tli), the skull rack. Thousands of skulls, bleached white by the sun, were arranged in orderly rows, staring at passersby through empty eye sockets. The headless bodies were then cut up and fed to the

Human sacrifice to make the crops grow. Captives were tied to wooden frames and shot with arrows in the belief that their blood, dripping onto the earth, would make it fertile. (Picture redrawn from the Codex Nuttall.)

animals in the Chief Speaker's zoo. The legs and arms, though, were saved and eaten at banquets. Unlike cannibals, who eat human flesh for nourishment, the Aztecs believed the flesh of those sacrificed to the gods had magical powers that passed into the person who ate them.

Heart-cutting was not the only form of human sacrifice. Priests drowned children in honor of Tlaloc; the more the frightened youngsters cried, the more rain he'd send, they believed. Slaves bought for the purpose were tied to high frames and riddled with arrows so that their dripping blood would enrich the soil and bring forth a bountiful crop. Those sacrificed to the fire god were given narcotics to dull pain and thrown into a bonfire. Slave women were beheaded as they danced to symbolize the gathering of the new maize crop.

Xipe Totec (She'e-pay totec) was honored in a grisly ceremony. This god ruled the springtime, when nature is reborn after the long sleep of the dry season, during which the earth is brown and cracked. He made the land fertile again, covering it with a fresh mantle of green, which, to the Aztec, resembled a new "skin." His name, in fact, means "Our Lord the Flayed One," that is, one who is skinned.

An exceptionally brave prisoner was led to a platform on top of which rested a round stone disk decorated with carvings of Xipe Totec. A rope that passed through the center of the disk was attached to the prisoner's waist, leaving him free to walk around the stone, but no further. There he stood, awaiting his fate, naked except for a loincloth and sandals.

A priest dressed as a bear came forward, followed by five warriors dressed in gorgeous feathered costumes and armed with the *maquauhuitl* (mah-kaw-wee-tl), the sword-club. The *maquauhuitl* was a fearsome weapon about the size and shape of a baseball bat, only flat, with wedges of

*The macquauitl,
or sword-club,
edged with wedges
of obsidian.*

obsidian glued into the edges on either side. Obsidian is a hard volcanic glass so sharp that it can behead a person with one blow.

The priest now handed the prisoner his "weapons": four light wooden clubs and a sword-club. The only problem was that the obsidian wedges in his *maquauhuitl* had been replaced with white feathers.

At the priest's signal, the first warrior advanced dancing, shield extended, weapon raised. The poor man on the stone threw his wooden clubs, which were easily turned aside by the shield. They then began the unequal contest with the sword-clubs. Some prisoners were so skilled that they wore out their attackers; those who survived were thought to be favored by Xipe Totec and freed with rich prizes. Few survived. At the slightest scratch, the prisoner was dragged away to have his chest cut open.

A priest then flayed the body, peeling off the whole skin in a single piece. Another priest put on the skin and danced through the streets, demanding gifts at every house along the way. None refused, because he had become the living image of "Our Lord the Flayed One." The rich gave costly feather capes, the poor handfuls of maze and tamales. Mothers placed their infants in the "god's" arms to be blessed.

There is no telling how many victims were sacrificed each year to the gods. Thousands must have died during *normal* times. On special occasions, however, the numbers were tremendous. At least twenty thousand, and maybe as many as fifty thousand, people died when the Great Temple of Huitzilopochtli and Tlaloc was dedicated in 1487. Captives waited their turn on the stone in four lines that stretched two miles across the city. Relays of priests needed four days to cut out their hearts, leaving Tenochtitlan to smell like a slaughterhouse for weeks afterward. Not only the capital, but every Aztec city and town had its ceremonies, each sacrificing according to its size and means.

Horrible as it was, we must remember that human sacrifice was not murder, which the Aztecs punished as a crime against the tribe. Sacrifice, to the Aztecs, was a spiritual act, a blessing, man's bowing to the all-powerful gods of nature. Victims were killed without hatred or anger, honored by their priest-executioners. This attitude, plus the fact that victims believed they were going straight to heaven, explains why so many fierce warriors went willingly to their deaths. We even know of warriors who demanded the "honor" of dying on the sacrificial stone.

The priests who performed these sacrifices were trained in the *Calmecac* schools. Everything they needed in order to serve the gods was taught by priests famous for their wisdom and faith. Many subjects had to be learned thoroughly before a young man became qualified to offer sacrifices: mathematics, astronomy, glyph reading and writing, religious poetry, music and dancing, magic, history, drug use, and the sacred ball game called *tlachtli* (tlatch-tlee).

Aztec games were not for recreation, but a form of worship carried out in front of important temples. *Tlatchtli*, a game played with a solid rubber ball weighing several pounds, was like basketball and soccer combined. It was played on a court with two walls with a stone hoop set vertically in each wall. The object of the game was to pass the ball through the hoop without touching it with the hands; only elbows, knees, hips, and buttocks could be used.

Two players test their skill in the sacred ball game. The object of the game was to send a heavy rubber ball through stone hoops, which projected inward at right angles to the side walls, without using the hands. Carved skulls watch the play, perhaps indicating that the loser lost everything, including his head, which wound up on the skull rack in the sacred precinct of Tenochtitlan. (Picture redrawn from the Magliabecchiano Codex.)

The heavy ball was dangerous at high speeds and players had to wear padded leather belts to protect their bodies. Even so, men were knocked cold, even killed, by a blow to the head or stomach. *Tlatchtli* was so difficult that the first team to score won the game and could take the spectators' clothes as a prize. In some games, the losing team may have been sacrificed to the gods.

Life in the *Calmecac* was harsh, for only through harshness could the future priests gain the self-control needed to serve the gods properly. Life was an endless round of fasts and penances in which youngsters drew blood from their own ears, lips, tongue, and legs as offerings to the idols. They often rose in the middle of the night to go into the mountains alone to pray and to bathe in freezing streams. *Calmecac* training was so thorough that, in addition to becoming priests, graduates were invited to join the governing classes. The Chief Speaker and the Snake Woman, his second-in-command, army generals, and judges were always *Calmecac* graduates.

∽　　∽　　∽

The priest's closest helper in serving the gods was the warrior. The Aztec idea of war was completely different from our own. We fear war, seeing it was a tragedy full of suffering and cruelty. The Aztecs, however, feared peace, seeing it as unnatural and a disaster for humanity. They lived for war as the highest good humans could achieve. War, they believed, was the law of the world, beautiful and necessary. It was the acting out of the drama in which Huitzilopochtli fought the darkness, conquered death, and saved the world. Without war, there couldn't be captives for sacrifice and no lifegiving blood for the gods. Strange as it seems to us, war, with all its terrors, was really a struggle for life, to the Aztecs. It was also a source of tribute and loot, their reward for such devoted service.

To fill those rare periods of peace between wars, the Aztecs invented the "War of Flowers," a sort of play-war, except that nobody laughed. Tenochtitlan arranged with its neighbors to send their best warriors to meet its own champions at a given time and place. The meeting's only purpose was to gain victims for sacrifice. Both sides fought and, when satisfied that they had enough captives, called off the battle, parting as the greatest of friends.

An Aztec boy was dedicated to war from the beginning. The moment he came into the world, a tiny shield and bow was placed in his hands as symbols of his role in life. Women relatives cradled the infant in their arms, tenderly whispering a prayer:

> Loved and tender son,
> This is the will of the gods.
> You are not born in your true house
> Because you are a warrior. Your land
> Is not here, but in another place.
> You are promised to the field of battle.
> You are dedicated to war.
> You must give the Sun your enemies' blood.
> You must feed the earth with corpses.
> Your house, your fortune, and your destiny
> Is in the House of the Sun.
> Serve, and rejoice that you may be worthy
> To die the Death of Flowers!

As he grew, he was given toy weapons; putting an arrow through a frog or bird brought his father's praise and a loving pat on the head. The boy memorized a short poem that explained his duty and what the tribe expected of him:

> There is nothing like death in war;
> Nothing like the flowery death
> So precious to Him who gives life!
> Far off I see it!
> My heart yearns for it!

The *Telpuchcalli* schools were attended by the sons of ordinary citizens who'd be neither priests nor governors, but follow their fathers' trades and go to war when necessary. Their instructors were respected warriors who knew how to get the best from others. They taught their pupils a little history, some religious songs, a couple of dances and a lot about fighting.

Much of the time was spent in toughening the boys mentally and physically. The idea was drummed into their heads that the warrior's death was to be welcomed, not feared. The Aztecs believed that going to heaven had nothing to do with living a good life, but dying well. A warrior killed in battle or captured and sacrificed had been chosen by the gods for a special privilege. Each morning, as the sky purpled in the east, Huitzilopochtli began the day's journey. Surrounded by fiery snakes, the sun's rays, he stepped into his glittering litter, the flaming disk of the sun, to be carried across the sky by the spirits of dead warriors. After four years with the sun, the warrior's spirit returned to earth as a hummingbird to live among the flowers, forever young, swift, and beautiful. Everyone else, except women who died in childbirth and had their own heaven, wandered through the eight hells beneath the earth. Their souls crossed raging rivers, passed between mountains that constantly rolled against each other, were lashed by obsidian-blade winds and attacked by ugly beasts before finding rest in the ninth hell.

Future warriors learned to be afraid only of being afraid. The greatest sin was cowardice, which disgraced him, his family, and his teachers. If a man was captured, he was expected to accept the consequences. Since the gods had selected him for capture, escaping was disobedience. Anyone who escaped and returned to Aztec territory was killed for defying the gods.

Telpuchcalli teachers deliberately made their pupils uncomfortable in order to harden their bodies for battle. The schoolday was filled with physical work such as carrying adobe bricks and forced marches up mountainsides under the broiling sun. And they drilled with weapons until their use became automatic.

The Aztecs were still a Stone Age people. Gold, silver and copper were used for ornaments, but they had not learned to work hard metal such as iron. Yet their weapons, though made of stone, obsidian and wood, could do fearful damage. In addition to the *maquauhuitl*, the favorite weapon of all tribes of the Valley of Mexico and the Gulf coast, the Aztecs were armed with spears from six to ten feet long and lightweight "darts" about four feet in length. The heavy spear could be thrown only by a strong man, but darts were hurled with the aid of the *atl-atl*, or dart-thrower. This was a flat piece of wood with a groove down the center in which the dart rested. One end of the *atl-atl* had a peg to hold the dart in place, plus a handle for the warrior to grip. The *atl-atl* was really an extension of the human arm that allowed darts to be hurled further and more accurately than with the arm alone. For longer distances, the Aztecs had slings, which flung round stones, and bows and arrows.

The warrior protected himself with a shield made of wood and animal hide, a wooden helmet, and body armor. The armor was made of thick layers of cotton padding and looked like a suit of long underwear. Lightweight and comfortable, it could withstand flint-tipped arrows and slashes with the sword-club.

Telpuchcalli boys fought mock battles that were as close to the real thing as possible without actually going out to kill; if captured, pricking with cactus needles and beatings took the place of sacrifice. Nevertheless, the

The atl-atl, or dart-thrower, for throwing short, lightweight spears long distances. The sample shown here is nearly five feet long.

weapons used in mock battles were sharp and few escaped without nasty cuts that scarred them for life. Scars were badges of honor, like medals imprinted permanently on the skin. Teachers encouraged pupils to take risks, for hard knocks made better warriors. Occasionally, an over-eager or careless youngster died. That, too, was all right, since the Hummingbird Wizard had a place for him at his right hand.

Telpuchcalli boys accompanied the army on its campaigns, seeing war first-hand. They stared wide-eyed as the gorgeously dressed warriors prepared for battle. Although the army had no uniforms, certain costumes were reserved for special groups of warriors. The more prisoners a warrior took, the more elaborate the costume he was entitled to wear. Famous warriors wore huge reed frames tied to their backs and decorated with feathers. These bursts of color—yellows, greens, blues, oranges, reds—swayed in the breeze or stood out like fans. Brightly colored paper streamers dangled from their weapons. Gold hung from their necks, while their arms were wrapped with bands of the same material. Plugs of precious jade and turquoise were stuck through holes in their ears, lips, and nostrils.

Warriors who belonged to the elite orders of Jaguar Knights and Eagle Knights tried to look like the animals they worshipped. A Jaguar Knight covered his body with the skin of a jaguar or ocelot, his head showing through the animal's jaws. The Eagle Knight covered his body with cotton armor studded with eagle feathers and wore a wooden helmet shaped like an eagle's head, complete with hooked beak. A knight wanted to be seen and recognized by everyone, friend or foe. Like a portable billboard, the costume advertised his rank and accomplishments, showing him to be a person worthy of respect.

The younger *Telpuchcalli* boys sat on the sidelines, taking in the color and excitement. First temple sacrifices, now the battlefield, got them used to hearing screams and seeing blood. There was plenty to hear and see.

The older boys fought alongside warriors assigned to look after them. The only way for an Aztec boy to become a man, and thus a full citizen, was to capture an enemy warrior for sacrifice. Killing him brought no honor, for the gods needed only the blood of the living. To deprive the gods of their "divine water" was to deprive war of its purpose, to make it meaningless.

A boy's head was shaved except for a pigtail that hung down the back. That pigtail was an insult to any spirited youngster, an announcement that he was still a child. Only a warrior who had taken a prisoner could cut off his pigtail. If he fought in three battles and still had his pigtail, anyone could insult him without fear of the law. His family was ashamed of him, and no father would consider him a fit husband for his daughter. A pigtail must have felt like a heavy ship's anchor to a seventeen-year-old.

Success in battle was the only way for a commoner to rise in the world. Warriors received no pay, but those who took prisoners were rewarded by the tribe. The more prisoners he took, the more land and booty he received. This system of reward-by-merit made it possible for a slave's son to become a general, ambassador, tax collector, or director of a school. A nobleman's son who failed to take a prisoner was ineligible for the lowest public office. He wasn't a man.

The Aztecs never began a war without warning the enemy of their intentions. Whenever the Chief Speaker and his council decided to expand the empire, they sent ambassadors to negotiate with the people concerned. The ambassadors carried an idol of Huitzilopochtli and a message: "Add this god to your temple." In addition, they demanded tribute, slaves, and sacrificial victims to be sent regularly to Tenochtitlan. In exchange, they promised to

In this statue, almost fifteen inches high, an Eagle Knight stares out from his headdress.

allow the country to live under its own rulers and laws, free from Aztec interference. And, of course, it would enjoy the "protection" of Hummingbird Wizard and his armies.

If the ruler refused, it was Huitzilopochtli, not the Aztecs, who was offended and demanded revenge. The great drum boomed atop the god's pyramid to summon the army. Every able-bodied man left work to join his unit in front of the clan's temple. Within twenty-four hours the Chief Speaker could gather a force of two hundred thousand warriors from Tenochtitlan, the provinces, and the allied cities of Texcoco and Tacuba.

The Mexicans had neither pack animals nor the wheel, which meant that everything had to be moved by human muscle power. Aztec armies traveled on foot, followed by thousands of porters, usually slaves and women, who carried supplies and set up camp. The army moved swiftly, silently; there was no joking, for war was a serious business and the gods had no sense of humor. Since the route passed through friendly territory at first, discipline was strict. Any warrior who broke ranks or stole food from the fields alongside the road was killed on the spot and his body displayed as an example to those who followed.

As soon as the army entered enemy territory, the general called its ruler to a final conference. He appeared on schedule, for although war was about to begin, it was in reality a religious ceremony whose rules had to be obeyed by both sides. If the ruler refused the last peace offer, the Aztecs gave him bundles of weapons to distribute among his warriors in case they didn't have enough of their own. The Aztecs didn't see anything strange about arming an enemy, for war was a judgment of the gods, who favored the right side regardless of weapons.

The Mexican Indians never went in for complicated tactics. Battles were arranged beforehand, so that each side could position its forces for a true test of the god's will.

At the general's signal, the Aztec ranks broke into shouts, howls, and war cries. Priests beat drums, blew conch-shell trumpets, and shook gourd rattles. Warriors blew bird-bone whistles, clashed weapons against shields, and did threatening dances. Noise had the important military purpose of helping the Aztecs work themselves into a fighting frenzy and making the enemy nervous.

The missilemen went into action first. Slingers let loose a hail of stones as bowmen filled the air with arrows. When they ran out of ammunition, the spearmen stepped forward, followed by swarms of warriors with the *atl-atl*. The main blow, however, was delivered toe-to-toe with the sword-club by the bulk of the army. As the battle line advanced, squads of priests with ropes followed in its tracks. Captives were tightly bound and sent to the rear. Wounded enemies were treated immediately by priest-doctors, for blood was too precious to be wasted.

Losing the battle meant losing the war. The Aztecs' aim was to burst into the enemy city and head for the temple square. The defenders, fighting under the eyes of their gods, fought until the Aztecs set fire to their temple. All resistance ended at the first sight of flames. The gods had decided. Either the local god had abandoned his people or been overpowered by Huitzilopochtli. No wonder the Aztec victory symbol was a burning temple pierced by an arrow. Another territory had been added to the empire. Another people would send tribute and slaves and sacrificial victims to Tenochtitlan. There seemed no stopping the Aztecs' march of conquest.

ᕲ   ᕲ   ᕲ

The Aztecs were a proud warrior people confident in their own strength and the power of their gods. Yet the shadows were lengthening, for at the moment of their greatest glory, their empire was doomed. They had no way of knowing it, but they were about to meet other warriors, equally proud and confident that they'd been given a mission by God— their One True God.

What had taken centuries to build, would be destroyed in just thirty months. Destroyed totally and forever.

2 Strangers from the Sunrise

⊙⊙

The waterfront, Havana, Cuba, February 1519.

A crowd of armed men surrounded Hernan Cortes, listening intently to his promises of fame and fortune. Although no one could know it then, he would become the most famous of *Conquistadores*, Spanish conquerors of the New World.

To see Cortes once was to remember him always. Something about him inspired confidence, setting him apart as a born leader. A tall man, lean and broad-shouldered, he had bowed legs that gave him a rolling gait. His face, grayish despite years in the tropical sunshine, contrasted with thick hair and beard of bluish-black.

Even in the humid heat, he dressed elegantly, in the style of a sixteenth-century gentleman: tight breeches, knee-length boots, starched shirt, sleeveless jacket, brimless hat. A long, needle-pointed sword hung at his hip in a velvet-covered scabbard. The scar under his lower lip testified that he was an old hand at swordplay.

Cortes at forty-five, at the height of his career as conqueror of Mexico. This portrait was painted in 1530 and still hangs in the Hospital Jesus Nazareno, which Cortes founded in Mexico City.

People sensed Cortes's inner strength not in his size or dress, but in his eyes and the way he carried himself. His eyes, gray and grave, seemed to bore into people, reading their secret thoughts. Yet no one could tell what went on behind those eyes, for he spoke little and kept his thoughts to himself. Not even his closest comrades, to whom he owed his life, knew what he'd do from one day to the next. His mind was always racing, always planning, always thinking ahead.

Cortes moved gracefully, with the assurance of one used to giving orders and being obeyed. Always in control of himself, he spoke politely to soldiers and servants, who addressed him with the greatest respect.

When he became angry, the veins in his throat bulged, his scar flared, but he never raised his voice. "Shut up" was his strongest expression. He said nothing when he was really angry, a sure sign that he was plotting revenge. He never forgot a favor, or forgave an insult.

Cortes knew what he wanted and how to get it. And God help anyone who stood in his way. He was utterly ruthless. No lie, no amount of cheating, no violence would prevent him from reaching his objective.

~ ~ ~

The future conqueror of Mexico was born in 1485, the only child of Catalina Pizarro Altamirano, a deeply religious woman, and Martin Cortes de Monroy, a retired army officer. The family owned some land in Medellin, a small town in the Spanish province of Extremadura, but it was far from wealthy. Money was always tight and the style of living simple.

Extremadura shaped Cortes as the sculptor's chisel shapes marble. Lying in the extreme western part of the country, Extremadura—"The Harsh, Remote Land"—is a bleak, uninviting plateau of small farms and great poverty.

Hardship has molded the people, making them tough, independent, and adventurous. Like other young *extremeños*, Cortes knew that he'd have to make his way in the world by himself; his family simply couldn't afford to support him at home. It is no accident that the sons of Extremadura should find their way to the New World, or that four other *Conquistadores* came from within a sixty-mile radius of Medellin: Vasco Nuñez de Balboa of Panama, Francisco Pizarro of Peru, Pedro de Valdivia of Chile, Hernando de Soto of Florida.

Little is known about Cortes's childhood except that he was sickly and that his parents wanted him to become a lawyer, a profession that might lead to service in the government of King Ferdinand and Queen Isabella. When he reached the age of fourteen, his parents scraped together enough money to send him to the University of Salamanca. People grew up quickly in those days, and fourteen was the normal age to begin university studies.

Cortes spent the next two years studying Latin, grammar, and law. But although he learned easily, his heart wasn't in school. He felt cramped, bored, restless. He wanted fame and wealth, not to spend his life in musty courtrooms.

He quit school and returned home, where there must have been a terrific row with his parents. They had scrimped and saved to give him an education, and now there was nothing to show for their trouble. Husband and wife told their son bluntly that he'd have to "seek his fortune"; that is, get out.

It so happened that his father's friend, Nicolas de Ovando, had recently been appointed governor of Hispaniola. Columbus had found the New World only nine years before and already Spanish settlements dotted Hispaniola, next to Cuba the largest of the Caribbean islands. Here a bold person might carve out an estate larger than anything back home. Ovando agreed to take Hernan along as a member of his staff, an important post that promised to fulfill his wishes.

Unfortunately, while Ovando's fleet was preparing to sail, Cortes fell into trouble. He'd gone to a house one night secretly to visit a young woman and, while walking along the wall near her bedroom window, it collapsed under his weight. Badly hurt and running a high fever, he missed the West Indian fleet. It wasn't until 1504 that he was well enough to sail from the bustling seaport of Seville. All he had with him were the clothes on his back, a sword and some dried fruit, a gift from his mother. He was nineteen, free, and on his own.

Upon landing in Hispaniola, he reported to Ovando's office. The governor was away, but his secretary greeted him warmly. As a settler, he said, Cortes was entitled to a parcel of land for farming and Indian slaves to do the work. Cortes, frowning, replied, "Land? I don't want land. I didn't come here to till the soil like a peasant. *I came for gold!*" A couple of weeks of hunger persuaded him to accept the land.

Cortes settled in the village of Azua near Santo Domingo, the island's capital. Life wasn't easy, even with slaves to do the work. He had little money and little to look forward to. His only entertainment was hunting and love affairs with local women, often leading to sword fights with rivals. One rival gave him the lip scar. What a bleak future stared him in the face! He was marooned for life, trapped, in effect, on a tropical island.

One night, after being in Azua for seven years, he dreamed that he was wearing rich clothes and eating his meals to the sound of trumpets. Strange, brown skinned people bowed deeply before him, addressing him as their prince. He awoke refreshed. His luck, he knew, was about to change.

Some days later, Governor Ovando ordered a wealthy landowner named Diego Velasquez to conquer the neighboring island of Cuba. Velasquez looked around for trustworthy men to help him and appointed Cortes as one of his captains. The Indians of Cuba proved no match for the invaders. They were easily defeated and their lands divided among the followers of Velasquez, who had been appointed governor of the island. Cortes received thousands of acres and scores of Indian slaves in payment for his part in the fighting.

Now everything he touched succeeded as if by magic. He introduced cattle into Cuba and before long had a valuable beef herd. Gold was found on his property. He became a magistrate in the city of Santiago. He wore gold buttons on his cloak, lived in a fine house, and had a secure future.

Yet his dissatisfaction grew. Deep down he felt that God had put him on earth to do marvelous, heroic things. What these things were he didn't know. That God would show him the way, he never doubted.

❧   ❧   ❧

Cortes's chance came in 1519, when he was thirty-four years old. The West Indies had a serious labor shortage. Spanish rule was so harsh that the Taino Indians, easygoing, peaceful people, were dying out, mostly from disease and overwork. Those who revolted were tracked down with hunting dogs and massacred or, worse, tortured to death as examples to others. Although Negro slaves would later replace the Indians, in the early 1500s Spaniards still hoped to find other Indians to enslave nearby.

In 1517 and 1518, Governor Velasquez sent out two small slave-catching expeditions. Both left Havana, sailing westward into uncharted waters. But instead of discovering other West Indian islands, they stumbled upon the Yucatan peninsula whose inhabitants, the Mayas, were anything but easygoing. Whenever the Spaniards landed, they were showered with stones, spears, and darts. Warriors swinging obsidian-edged clubs charged them fearlessly. Dozens of Spaniards died and nearly all their comrades were wounded.

Only the Indians of Tabasco along the southern shore of the Gulf of Mexico were friendly and eager to trade. The Spaniards noticed that the Tabascans lived in large towns with stone buildings. And they wore golden jewelry. The sight of the yellow metal set their hearts pounding. When Juan de Grijalva, leader of one of the expeditions, asked in sign language where the gold came from, the Indians pointed toward the western mountains and repeated "Mexico, Mexico." Whenever they used this word they bowed deeply, seeming to shake with fear. "Mexico" and "gold" immediately became locked together in the Spaniards' minds.

Governor Velasquez decided to send another expedition to get to the bottom of the riddle. Since his duties prevented him from leading it in person, he needed someone to go in his place. That person had to be a good soldier, efficient, and above all loyal. If he found Mexico, Velasquez meant to claim the country for King Charles, grandson of Ferdinand and Isabella, Spain's new ruler, along with a generous portion of the treasure. The expedition's leader, being merely a hired hand, would be entitled to nothing beyond his salary. If he failed, or died, Velasquez would simply write off the expedition as a bad investment. He couldn't lose either way, he thought.

The governor asked Hernan Cortes to lead this third expedition. Cortes was one of the leading men in Cuba, but not influential enough to rival his chief, who had friends in the court of King Charles. Cortes seemed the ideal choice, especially since he went out of his way to be friendly and helpful to the governor. Velasquez was to regret his decision for the rest of his life.

Cortes had no intention of risking his neck while the governor sat comfortably in Cuba. As soon as he received his commission as captain-general of the expedition, he began to act as an independent leader. He went about with a heavy gold chain around his neck, imitating a high government official. He scoured the island for ships to hire and supplies to buy. Don Hernan had such faith in himself that he sank every peso he owned into the expedition; he even went into debt, mortgaging his lands to pay for the supplies. Here was the chance of a lifetime, and he meant to grab it with both hands.

Cortes visited seacoast towns and backcountry settlements to recruit fighting men. He knew the type of men he wanted—*Conquistadores*. These were not ordinary men, but a type that would become famous throughout the Americas during the next century. They were young, mostly in their twenties and early thirties. Experienced soldiers, nearly all had fought Indians in the islands; about half were veterans of Spain's wars against the French and Turks. But most important of all, they had an inner strength born of confidence in the righteousness of their cause.

Conquistadores believed that what they did was right. One of them was Bernal Diaz del Castillo, the soldier-author whose *True History of the Conquest of New Spain* is an eyewitness account of Cortes's wars. "We came here," said Diaz, "to serve God and also to get rich." He and his comrades never doubted that they were soldiers of God, crusaders in the New World.

Spain is the home of the crusade, the Christian holy war against infidels, unbelievers. When Muslims from North Africa overran Spain in the early 700s, the Christians began a crusade to liberate their homeland. The crusading idea spread to the rest of Europe, which sent vast armies to drive the Muslims out of the Holy Land, Palestine. Although these crusades failed, the Spaniards finally defeated the Muslims in 1492, the year Columbus sailed and Cortes celebrated his seventh birthday.

Columbus's discoveries spread the crusading idea worldwide. Spaniards believed that God commanded them to conquer infidels everywhere. Conquering them was really merciful, they believed, because it brought them the Christian religion and the chance to save their souls from hell. And since *Conquistadores* fought in God's name, it was only fair that they should take others' wealth in return for their efforts. Cortes's *Conquistadores* could hope for no wages apart from their God-given rewards—loot. "Holy bandits" is what one Indian chief called them.

By February, 1519, Cortes had eleven ships, one hundred sailors, and five hundred eight soldiers. This tiny force was far more dangerous that it seemed at first glance. The army's backbone was its detachments of foot-soldiers, each armed with its special weapon. The swordsmen, the largest unit, carried weapons made in Toledo, Spain, of the finest steel in the world; each blade was a yard long, double-edged, razor-sharp and needle-pointed.

It is said that this sword of Toledo steel, now in the Royal Armory, Madrid, belonged to Cortes.

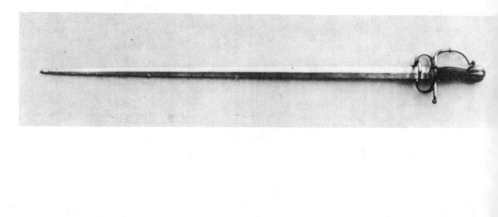

The halberd (left) combined two weapons: A hook for pulling an enemy to the ground and a heavy axe able to cut through even the toughest armor. The pike (right) was a steel-pointed spear, often twelve to fifteen feet long. Masses of pikemen working together acted like a steamroller on the battlefield.

Their comrades, the halberdiers, had seven-foot poles tipped with a steel spike and a huge axe blade. A strong man swinging a halberd became a human buzz-saw, mowing down anyone in his path. Pikemen used ashwood spears twelve feet long and too heavy to be thrown. These soldiers just came on in rows, pikes lowered, advancing behind a tidal wave of steel-tipped death.

The army's firepower came from thirty-two crossbow-men, thirteen musketeers, and the crews of fourteen light cannon made of brass or iron bars welded onto hoops. The crossbow was a short bow fixed crosswise to a stock and powered by twisted strings released by a trigger. This

Small-caliber cannon of the sort used by the Spaniards during the conquest of Mexico. Guns of this sort were not made of a single piece of metal, but of iron bars held in place by hoops. Instead of firing metal cannonballs, their ammunition was rounded stones shaped to fit each individual weapon.

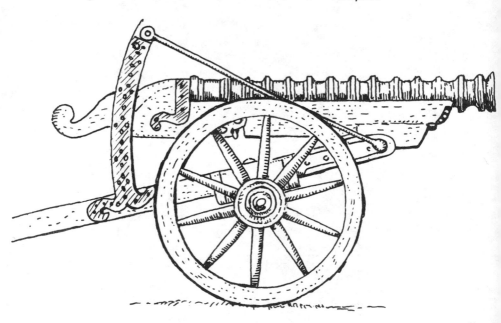

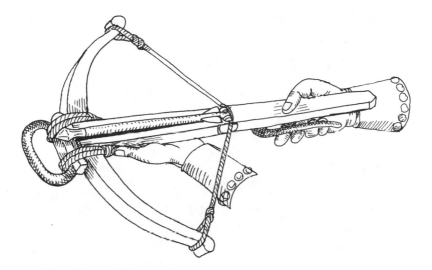

A crossbow could shoot an arrow, called a quarrel, short distances with the speed of a bullet.

weapon was so powerful that it could send a short, steel-pointed arrow called a "quarrel" through a suit of armor. Muskets and cannon outdistanced and hit harder than anything thrown with the human arm or propelled by strings.

The expedition's sixteen horses were its "tank" corps. Horses, as you know, are not native to the New World and had to be brought from Europe. In Cortes's day, they were still scarce and expensive, worth at least the price of fifty slaves apiece. Yet they were worth any price. Horses allowed scouts to cover large distances quickly, helping the army avoid ambushes. In battle they gave the army mobility and hitting power. Again and again, as we'll see, Cortes's cavalry plowed through swarms of Indian warriors without losing a man. Everyone in the army knew each horse by name and, whenever one died, mourned its loss like a dear friend's.

Men and horses wore armor. Soldiers gleamed in

polished steel helmets, breastplates, and armpieces. Horses wore large, square shields of wood and leather across their flanks, together with steel face masks.

Governor Velasquez became more suspicious as Cortes's force grew. Cortes seemed too self-confident, too set on having his own way. Once the fleet sailed, he could snap his fingers at the governor's orders and do as he pleased. At last Velasquez sent word that Cortes was to be arrested.

Cortes, who had taken the precaution of bribing the governor's secretary, learned of his plans immediately. If he was ever to achieve greatness, he knew he had to act before Velasquez's officers came to haul him off to jail. He gathered his men about him on the Havana waterfront. Their weapons glistened in the sun as he stood on a packing case, scanning the crowd. His eyes moved from face to face, fixing their attention, staring, probing, searching.

His speech was a stirring appeal to his men to serve themselves by serving God. From the beginning, he made it clear that, wherever Mexico was, he intended to conquer it. "Certain it is, my friends and companions, that every good man of spirit desires and strives to make himself the equal of the excellent men of his day and even those of the past. And so I am embarking upon a great and beautiful enterprise, which will be famous in time to come, because I know in my heart that we shall take vast and wealthy lands. We are waging a just and good war which will bring us fame. Almighty God, in whose name it will be waged, will give us victory. I offer you great rewards, although they will be wrapped about with great hardships. If you do not abandon me, as I shall not abandon you, I shall make you the richest men who every crossed the seas. You are few, I see, but such is your spirit that no Indians will prevail against you, for we have seen how God has favored the Spanish nation in these parts."

An officer then unfurled the expedition's banner, designed by Cortes and embroidered by a woman in town. It had white and blue flames with a golden cross in the middle. Around the margins was a Latin motto, meaning, "Friends, let us follow the Cross, and with true faith in this symbol we shall conquer."

The fleet sailed soon after, on the outgoing tide. Cortes's crusade had begun. It was February 10, 1519.

～　　～　　～

The first landfall was Cozumel, an island off the eastern coast of Yucatan. The vessels anchored in the shallows and Cortes sent the troops ashore while sailors made repairs. The *Conquistadores* appreciated the stopover after a week of sleeping on rough planks jammed together in the small, leaky ships.

They were going about their camp chores when a man beached his canoe nearby. Almost naked, his body bronzed by the sun, he seemed like an Indian from the distance. But when he came closer and saw they were Europeans, he fell on his knees, crossed himself, and burst into tears.

After calming him with soft words and strong wine, the soldiers listened to his story in stunned silence. His name was Jeronimo de Aguilar, and he was a Spaniard who had been shipwrecked on the Yucatan coast eight years earlier. The Mayas had quickly rounded up his shipmates, sacrificing some and fattening up the others in cages to be eaten at their feasts. Aguilar escaped with his life, only to be enslaved. After being traded several times, he was bought by a kindly village chief who took a liking to him and set him free.

Aguilar's only tie with home was a tattered prayer book, which he read every day to remind him that he was a Christian in a pagan land. He'd lost hope of ever seeing his people again when word came that enormous white-

◎◎ CORTES IN THE

BAJA CALIFORNIA

Gulf of California

Sea of Cortes

Approximate Boundary of New Spain 1535

GULF OF

MEXICO
Otumba

Tenochtitlan
(Mexico City)

Tlaxcala

Cholula

MT. POPOCATEPETL

TOTONACS

Villa Rica de la Vera
Cruz

MECS

TABASCO

R. Grijalva

Oaxaca

ZAPOTACS

PACIFIC OCEAN

AZTEC LANDS

ROUTE of CORTES
- - - - - 1520
————— 1535

0   100   200   300 *miles*
0   100   200   300   400 *Kilometers*

NEW WORLD

ATLANTIC OCEAN

MEXICO

Havana Trinidad CUBA HISPANIOLA
Azua

Cape Catoche Santiago
de Cuba Santo
Domingo

YUCATAN COZUMEL IS.

JAMAICA

MAYAS CARIBBEAN SEA

R. Sarstun

GUATEMALA
HONDURAS

winged "birds"—sailing ships—were swimming in the sea off Cozumel. Rescued at last, he gladly joined the expedition, lending it his skill as an interpreter of the local Indian languages.

The fleet left Cozumel on a northerly course around the tip of Yucatan. Hugging the coastline, always in sight of land, it came to the mouth of the Rio Grijalva, named by the leader of the earlier expedition in his own honor. A lot had happened since his visit the previous year. Neighboring tribes had called the Tabascans cowards and women for trading with the strangers. The appearance of Cortes now gave them the chance to wipe away these insults.

The Spaniards found the Indians lined up on the beach, whooping it up and eager for a fight. When Aguilar explained that they came in friendship, a chief drove his spear into the ground, warning that they'd attack the moment the strangers advanced beyond the palm trees.

Cortes preferred to gain his objectives by peaceful means, avoiding bloodshed whenever possible. The Tabascan challenge, however, gave him no choice. He had to fight to keep the loyalty of his own men, who respected only a winner. Fighting was also an investment in the future, a way of preventing even costlier battles. Word of the Tabascans' defeat, he knew, would quickly spread throughout the country, a warning to others that his little army could take care of itself.

Cortes landed his troops and captured Tabasco city, the tribal capital, after a short, sharp fight. But instead of begging for peace, as he'd hoped, the Indian army withdrew into the countryside and called for reinforcements from inland towns. The Tabascans were gearing up for an all-out, winner-take-all fight.

On the morning of March 13, 1519, thirteen days after landing, the Spaniards awoke to find the plain in front of them a sea of swaying feathers.

No fewer than forty thousand Indians were drawn up in battle array. Here, at eighty to one, were odds to test the skill of any commander.

Cortes now showed himself to be a leader of genius. Coolly, as if observing things from above, he analyzed the situation. Great danger also meant great opportunity, to him. When outnumbered, he believed it best to do the unexpected, to attack, to throw the enemy off balance.

Cortes divided his army into two units. The infantry marched onto the plain to face the enemy, their flanks, or the side of their column, covered by crossbowmen, musketeers, and cannoneers. The commander, meanwhile, set out unobserved with the cavalry on a wide circle toward the enemy rear.

The Spaniards advanced with drums beating, trumpets blaring, and banner snapping in the breeze. For the first time on the American mainland, Spanish infantry were charging into battle.

A war cry heard so often in Europe burst from their ranks. *"Santiago! Santiago y a ellos!"* they shouted, calling upon Spain's patron saint for victory. "Saint James! Saint James and at them!"

"Alala! Alala!" the Tabascans replied as they rushed to meet them.

Within minutes the Spaniards were surrounded by their enemies. Warriors, their faces painted in black and white stripes, screamed, whistled, howled, and beat their drums.

This meeting outside Tabasco city set the pattern for all Cortes's battles. The Spaniards, though heavily outnumbered, were superior to their enemies in every other way. Numbers alone have never brought victory. The Mexican Indian was a brave warrior, the Spaniard a disciplined soldier. There is a difference. The warrior fought not as part of a team with an overall plan, but as an individual for personal glory. Although he marched to battle in an orderly formation, his chiefs lost control of their men once the fighting began. The Indians became a surging, pushing mass that depended on numbers and fighting spirit to bring victory. If victory didn't come quickly, or if a chief was killed, the warriors fled in panic.

Not the Spaniards. They were true soldiers, members of a fighting team trained to work together and help each other. No matter how badly a battle went, they kept their ranks, obeying the orders of their officers or his second or third in command; orders were shouted or given by drum roll and trumpet call. When surrounded, they formed a hollow square, wounded in the center, fighting back to back until they or the enemy collapsed.

There were plenty of wounded to protect as a hail of Tabascan stones, arrows, and darts blanketed the small army. Yet Spanish discipline and weaponry soon began to tell. Crossbow quarrels shattered wooden shields, scattering splinters red with blood. Cannon belched fire, their stone balls cutting long avenues through the Indian mass. But it was the swordsmen who, standing toe-to-toe with the Indians, took the brunt of the action. The *maquauhuitl* was no match for the Spanish blade. The sword-club had no point, which meant it could only be used for slashing and chopping. To deliver a blow, the warrior had to lift his weapon, thereby uncovering his face and body. The sword, however, was like a boxer's fists, kept close to the body and used only when the enemy lowered his guard. Most Indians were killed with short, lightning sword jabs to the body or throat.

Despite their advantages, the Spaniards couldn't hold out indefinitely against such odds. The number of wounded increased, while their comrades grew tired. They were beginning to mutter when the sound of hoofbeats rose above the din of battle.

"Santiago! Santiago y a ellos!"

The cavalry plowed into the enemy from behind at a fast gallop. The combined weight of horse and rider, over a ton, tossed warriors into the air by twos and threes, like rag dolls. Horsemen thrust spears into Indians' faces or slashed with heavy swords, sending severed heads rolling in the dust.

But it was the horses themselves that were the winning weapon. The Tabascans had never seen such beasts before. They thought the horses were supernatural creatures and, at first, that animal and rider were one monstrous god out

Cortes's horses were the most important weapons in the conquest of Mexico, serving as the "tank corps" of his little army. (Redrawn from the Codex Florentino.)

to destroy them. Overcome by panic, they dropped their weapons and ran away, leaving eight hundred dead on the battlefield; the Spaniards had two killed and about fifty wounded.

The *Conquistadores* spent the rest of the day tending to their wounded. Facing an army surgeon required as much courage as standing up to the enemy. There were no such things as painkillers or antibiotics to prevent infection in the sixteenth century. Wounds were "seared"; that is, the soldier bit down on a lead musket ball while the surgeon burned the wound closed with a red-hot dagger blade. We still use the term "biting the bullet" for having to put up with anything unpleasant. Melted fat taken from the body of a dead Indian was then used to soothe the raw wound. End of treatment.

Next day, Tabascan chiefs came to the Spanish camp to ask for peace. As a peace offering, they gave Cortes gifts of food and jewelry; his horses, which they still feared, were offered bunches of roses. They also brought twenty slave girls to cook the officers' food, mend their clothes, and make themselves useful in other ways.

Among the slave girls was the tall, dignified nineteen-year-old who'd become the most famous woman in Mexican history. She was called Malinali, or "Princess of Suffering," a name that accurately described her life until then. Malinali, the daughter of a village chief, was born in southern Mexico. Her father died when she was still a child, her mother remarrying soon afterward. A son was born and the mother, fearing that Malinali might prevent her half-brother's becoming chief, sold her to traveling slave traders, who resold her in Tabasco.

Malinali suffered much, but also learned much during her years in slavery. Not only did she speak the Mayan language of the coastal Indians, she was fluent in "the pleasant sound," the Nahuatl of the inland peoples. She

The Conquistadores believed that they were not only out to take the Indians' wealth, but that they were crusaders fighting for Christianity. In this drawing from the Codex Florentino, an Indian offers the soldier's horse something to eat.

could translate Nahuatl into Maya, which Aguilar re-translated into Spanish. Once she learned Spanish for herself, she became Cortes's chief interpreter and, in time, his lover, bearing him a son named Martin in honor of Cortes's father.

Malinali was the first Mexican to become a Christian, taking the name Marina. *Conquistadores* called her Doña Marina, because she truly was a Most Honorable Lady. Indians always spoke of Cortes as Malinche, "Marina's captain." She was completely loyal to her captain and saved his army from destruction at least once. No matter how good a soldier he was, Cortes probably never could have conquered Mexico without her help. For not only did she tell him what the Indians were saying, but what they were thinking as well.

～　　～　　～

The fleet sailed from Tabasco, continuing up the coast until it reached the island of San Juan de Ulua, opposite the present city of Veracruz. Without realizing it, the *Conquistadores* had crossed an invisible border. For across the narrow channel on the mainland lay the easternmost outposts of the Aztec empire. Within hours of their arrival, messengers were racing across the mountains, bound for Tenochtitlan. The Chief Speaker, Montezuma II, had to be told about these strangers from the sunrise.

Montezuma, who became Chief Speaker in 1502 at the age of thirty-five, was the most powerful and learned of all Aztec rulers. His name, meaning "Angry Young Lord," was well-earned. A courageous general, he led his armies in person, expanding the empire in every direction. The tribute rolls grew each year, as more peoples sent their wealth to the city in the lake. As the empire's chief priest, he led the sacrificing in front of the temples, cutting out victims' hearts until he fell exhausted.

Yet Montezuma was unusual even for an Aztec priest. He'd spend hours alone each day poring over sacred books and brooding about religious matters. Were the people too lax in their prayers? Why had a temple mysteriously caught fire? The Chief Speaker always had the same explanation and cure: the gods were displeased and demanded more blood. Under his rule the number of sacrifices outgrew anything known in the past. He drove the priests to invent new ceremonies, better rituals for bloodletting. At his coronation over five thousand people were sacrificed. Even his dreams were deadly. He once awoke in the middle of the night to order his children's teachers and servants, hundreds of people, killed by sunrise. His subjects trembled as bearers carried him through the streets on his litter. No one, not even the highest nobleman, dared look him in the face for fear of being killed. Yet they obeyed his orders, believing that the gods told him what was best for the well-being of the tribe.

Montezuma II, the most powerful of the Aztec Chief Speakers, as seen by an artist of the 1600s.

News of the strangers sent a shiver through the Chief Speaker. For all his power, Montezuma was no freer than the captives awaiting sacrifice in wooden cages. The Angry Young Lord of the Aztecs was actually a slave himself, not to other men, but to the fears and superstitions that haunted his mind. These dominated his life and prevented him from thinking clearly. In the end they destroyed him and ruined his people.

Montezuma's worst fears seemed to be coming true. Mexico was the Aztecs' entire universe. They couldn't imagine that other people, so different from themselves, could exist anywhere else, let alone across the great salt waters to the east and west. Strange happenings had to be supernatural, magical. And strange beings resembling people had to be gods or their servants. It was all quite clear, to his way of thinking.

News of the strangers reminded Montezuma of an ancient legend. The legend concerned Quetzelcoatl (Ka'yt-zal-co-atl), one of the creator gods, mightier even than Hummingbird Wizard. He was God of Wisdom, Creator of the Calendar, and Inventor of Farming; it was he who brought maize to man by turning himself into an ant to steal it from that hardworking creature's secret hoard. Quetzelcoatl welcomed beautiful butterflies and birds sacrificed in his honor, but was horrified at human sacrifice.

Legend said that demons drove Quetzelcoatl from Mexico with evil magic. He fled with his loyal followers to the edge of the salt water in the east, where they boarded a raft of writhing, intertwined snakes and set out for a mysterious place beyond the horizon. But before leaving, he promised to return in the year One Reed—1519 in the European calendar. He'd then overthrow those who disobeyed his rule against human sacrifice and sit upon the throne of Mexico till the end of time.

Quetzelcoatl could do whatever he wished, even change his form. Carvings at Teotihuacan show him as

A statue, almost eighteen inches high and made of green stone, shows Quetzelcoatl, God of Wisdom, whom Montezuma thought had returned in the form of Cortes.

the Feathered Serpent, a snake with gaping jaws and feathers, instead of scales, covering his body. It was also said that he appeared sometimes as a white-skinned man with a beard of bluish-black.

Montezuma called five trusted advisers, all Jaguar Knights, to his palace. His orders, he explained, had to be followed to the letter on pain of death to themselves and their families. They must locate the strangers' "water houses" and meet their leader. They must watch his every movement, remember his every word, and report back to

Montezuma's ambassadors dive overboard as a Spanish soldier fires a musket. For a long time, Indians, who knew nothing of gunpowder, panicked whenever the invaders let off their weapons of lightning and thunder. (Redrawn from the Codex Florentino.)

him at any hour of the day or night. Pausing, he motioned for servants to bring the gifts they were to deliver in his name. They were presents worthy of a god: gold jewelry, strings of precious stones, a headdress of quetzel feathers, a crown of jaguar skin, a shield set with bands of gold alternating with rows of large pearls.

The Jaguar Knights and their porters, who carried the treasure in baskets on their heads, hurried to the coast where they boarded a richly decorated war canoe. Rowers made the craft fly over the water until they saw the strangers' vessels rising from the sea in the distance.

Doña Marina welcomed them aboard the flagship in the name of her captain. When they saw Cortes, they fell to their knees and kissed the deck in front of his feet. Rising, they dressed him in the finery of Quetzelcoatl.

Cortes stood still for the ceremony, while his men looked on. When it was over, he scowled and asked, "Is this all? Is this your gift? Is this the way you greet guests?"

"This is all, our lord," the Jaguar Knights replied.

Cortes put on his fiercest expression and had a cannon fired to show his displeasure. The gun's kick and roar sent the Aztecs sprawling onto the deck in a faint. After the Spaniards revived them, they leaped into their canoe, shouting to the rowers, "Faster, faster! Nothing must happen to us, until we report what we have seen!"

Cortes watched them go. His anger had only been pretended, an excuse for showing that he commanded the cannon's lightning and thunder, which he knew would be reported to Montezuma. He was pleased to think the gifts were only a down payment on the treasure awaiting him inland.

The Jaguar Knights were brought to Montezuma as soon as they returned to Tenochtitlan. He ordered the palace guards to wake him, even from a sound sleep, the moment they arrived.

The Angry Young Lord met them, not in the royal bedroom, but in the Hall of the Snake, a holy place nearby. Before listening to their report, he sacrificed a slave with his own hands and sprinkled them with his blood. Some of the servants present that night later told the Spanish priest and historian, Bernardino de Sahagun, what was said. The Jaguar Knights described the cannon, how it roared, belched fire, and spat out a ball that splintered a tree on the shore.

Nothing like these strangers had ever been seen in the world, they continued. "All iron was their war array. They clothed themselves in iron. They covered their heads with iron. Iron were their swords. Iron were their crossbows. Iron were their shields. Iron were their lances.

"And their deer, which bore them upon their backs, were as high as roof-tops.

"And they covered all parts of their bodies. Alone to be seen were their faces—very white. They had yellow hair, although the hair of some was black. Long were their beards.

"And their dogs [greyhounds and mastiffs] were very large. They had ears doubled over; great, hanging jowls; blazing eyes—flaming yellow, fiery yellow eyes; thin flanks, with ribs showing. They were very tall and fierce. They went about panting, with tongues hanging."

When Montezuma heard this report, an Indian recalled, "he was filled with fright. It was as if his heart fainted, as if his heart shriveled."

It was true. The blackbeard who commanded lightning and thunder was Quetzelcoatl. All the pieces of the puzzle fit. Had Montezuma thought otherwise, he would have sent the full power of Mexico, two hundred thousand warriors, eager to go to the sun with Huitzilopochtli, to crush the intruders. But he didn't dare challenge a god.

There was still a chance to save his throne and empire.

As chief priest, Montezuma was learned in the ways of the gods. Since they resembled humans in so many ways, they could be defeated by bribery and magic. He decided to try both, in the hope of persuading "Quetzelcoatl" to return to his realm in the east.

Montezuma now sent to the coast a large delegation led by Tendile, one of his most trusted officers. Delegation members were commanded to do whatever the "god" wanted, even allow themselves to be eaten, if that was his pleasure; they needn't worry about their families, since the state would take care of them.

Tendile found the strangers camped on the beach opposite San Juan de Ulua. The Spaniards were startled to see four thousand Indians suddenly emerge from among the trees and approach them. They came unarmed, decked out in fine clothes and jewels. Tendile led the way, followed by priests swinging containers of burning incense, whose clouds of pungent smoke resembled the cloud-land inhabited by the gods. Upon reaching the camp, servants set out a splendid banquet of turkeys, eggs, fruit, maize cakes, tortillas, and tamales of many kinds.

The Spaniards' mouths watered, for they had been living on a diet of stale ship's biscuit and pickled beef. But as Cortes and his officers sat down to eat, they were shocked to see priests throw a slave on his back, cut out his heart, and sprinkle his blood over the meal. They were honoring their guests with "divine water" and testing them at the same time.

The Spaniards became ill at the sight. They spat on the ground. They shook their heads and rolled their eyes, tears streaming down their cheeks. Montezuma's magicians, watching from the sidelines, were shaken. Quetzelcoatl, they knew, was also horrified at human sacrifice. Their magic was useless against the God of Wisdom.

Another, unbloodied, meal was brought, and when his

The Conquistadores arrive on the coast of Mexico. This picture of the event was one drawn by an Indian artist about thirty years later to illustrate Bernardino de Sahagun's account of Aztec life and how it was changed by Cortes. (Picture from the Codex Florentino.)

guests had eaten their fill, Tendile ordered the gifts brought forward. The Spaniards stared, hardly believing what they saw. Here were treasures beyond their wildest dreams. There was a helmet overflowing with gold dust and golden figurines of animals, birds, fish, and seashells. The

soldiers gasped when Tendile uncovered the most wonderful gift of all—two disks four fingers thick, each the size
of a large cartwheel. The first disk was of solid gold
etched with symbols of the sun. Its mate was of pure silver
with engravings representing the moon.

Now came Tendile's turn to be amazed. Cortes gave
him a wooden chair, some clothing and a handful of
colored glass beads for his master. Montezuma had been
so generous, he added, that he intended to visit his capital
to thank him personally and tell him about the Christian
religion. Montezuma might believe what he wished about
Cortes being the god Quetzelcoatl, but he could never
pretend to be anything other than a Christian man. To
have tried to impersonate the god would have been a sin
in the eyes of his church. Cortes was capable of lying about
many things, but not about his religious beliefs.

Tendile returned a week later with more gold and a
message from Montezuma. The road to Tenochtitlan, he
explained, was long and dangerous, and there wasn't
enough food in the city to feed such honored visitors. It
would be best if the "god" and his servants took the gifts
and sailed away in their water houses.

The Angry Young Lord still couldn't understand that
the strangers would never be satisfied with presents. Cortes
spoke the truth when he told Tendile, "We Spaniards suffer
from a disease of the heart which can only be cured by
gold." The more gold Montezuma sent, the more "heart
medicine" the Spaniards craved, and the more determined
they were to go to its source.

ᔍ   ᔍ   ᔍ

Cortes knew *what* he had to do, but not *how* to do it. He
had no idea where "Mexico" might be, except that it lay
to the west in a lake in a valley surrounded by mountains.
It would be foolish to plunge into an unknown country

with a handful of soldiers to search for the mysterious city. He needed allies to fight alongside his *Conquistadores*. He needed porters to carry their supplies, saving the men's energy for fighting. Most of all, he needed guides and information.

Cortes had none of these until a hot summer morning in July, 1519, when guards brought him five Indians found walking along the beach toward their camp. Upon questioning by Doña Marina and Aguilar, it was found that they weren't Aztecs, but Totonacs from the city of Cempoala, a day's march up the coast. The men were messengers from the Totonacs' high chief, sent to invite the Spaniards to visit his city.

Cempoalans filled the streets and crowded the rooftops to get a glimpse of the strangers. Smiling women offered them baskets of food, while children showered them with flower petals. The high chief, whom the Spaniards called the Fat Chief, because he weighed over four hundred pounds, was brought to meet Cortes on a litter and helped to stand by servants holding him on either side. Cortes hugged him warmly, if only halfway, as his arms weren't long enough to encircle him completely.

The Fat Chief explained that the Totonacs, a tribe inhabiting fifty large towns, had recently fallen under Aztec control. Like hungry coyotes, Montezuma's tribute collectors were picking the country clean. He wept openly as he told of sending hundreds of youths, boys and girls, each year to the bloodstained altars of Tenochtitlan.

The Fat Chief's complaints were music to Cortes's ears. Suddenly he realized that Montezuma didn't rule a united people, but an empire filled with sullen, vengeful subjects. At once his strategy became clear: divide and conquer. He'd play on the subject peoples' resentments to separate them from the empire, winning them as allies for his own purposes. One way or another, he meant to destroy the

Aztec empire and rule it as a territory under the king of Spain.

Cortes's chance came a few days after arriving in Cempoala. He was speaking to the Totonac leaders when a servant brought word that Montezuma's tribute collectors had just come into town. The Totonacs turned pale and ran to greet their unexpected visitors.

The five Mexicans wore richly embroidered cloaks and loincloths. Each had a crooked staff in one hand and a bouquet of roses in the other, which he made a great show of sniffing. Cortes and his men lined the town square to see the sight, but the tribute collectors turned up their noses and walked by as if they didn't exist.

Yet they weren't as calm as they seemed. After eating, they gave the Fat Chief a tongue-lashing for welcoming the strangers against their master's wishes. As a punishment, they demanded twenty Totonac children for immediate sacrifice.

Cortes saw his opportunity and took it. As soon as he learned of their demand, he told the Fat Chief to arrest the Mexicans. There was nothing to fear, he explained, for the Spanish army would stand behind its friends. The Fat Chief, who had heard of the Tabascans' defeat, found his courage. The tribute collectors were tied hand and foot to long poles and carried through the streets amid laughing crowds. In the meantime, runners spread news of the rebellion to the other Totonac towns.

Having begun the rebellion, Cortes meant to finish it in his own way. That night he secretly freed the captives, telling them to inform Montezuma of his love and respect. As for the Totonacs, he had them in the palm of his hand. For only his troops now stood between them and the Angry Young Lord's revenge. Like it or not, they had become his ally.

～ ～ ～

Cortes had one last problem to attend to before striking inland. From the moment he'd left Cuba, his every action was illegal. Velasquez, as governor of Cuba, was the king's representative; his orders had the same force as if they were written by King Charles himself. By sailing against those orders, Cortes had branded himself an outlaw. Anyone, even his own men, could hang him on the spot without a trial, as they would an ordinary pirate.

Cortes now showed that he hadn't wasted his time at the University of Salamanca. He'd learned that under Spanish law a group of men, whether at home or in the colonies, could found a town and elect their own government if they obtained the king's consent. The officers of the town government would then be responsible directly to the king and no one, not even a royal governor, could give them orders.

Carefully, so as to make it seem like their own idea, Cortes persuaded his captains to demand that the camp be turned into a town with the army as its citizens. These officers had all been chosen in Cuba for their fighting ability and loyalty to Cortes. Among them were Pedro de Alvarado, Cortes's second-in-command, Cristobal de Olid, Alonso de Avila, Juan Velasquez de Leon, and Juan de Escalante. At twenty-two, Gonzalo de Sandoval was the youngest captain. Cortes called him *"Hijo,"* son, for he loved him as his own child.

Before long the camp was buzzing with the idea. At a public meeting the soldiers insisted that they serve directly under the king, not Governor Velasquez. Cortes let himself be "persuaded." Instantly the shabby camp became a Spanish town with the grand name Villa Rica de la Vera Cruz—The Rich Town of the True Cross. Its soldier-citizens promptly elected the town councillors and officials; Cortes, naturally, was chosen governor and commander of the army.

Cortes wrote a long letter to King Charles, addressing him as "Very High, Very Powerful, and Most Excellent Prince, Very Catholic and Invincible Emperor, King and Lord." The letter explained his actions, asserting his loyalty and desire only to expand the Spanish empire and add to His Majesty's glory. This letter, the first of five sent during the next year, is one of our best sources of information about Cortes's activities.

Cortes' strongest argument, however, wasn't words on paper or a town outlined on sand dunes. He knew that the king, like himself, suffered from the same disease of the heart. In a rousing speech he persuaded his men to give up their share of the treasure as a gift to the king. The whole treasure, plus the letter, were entrusted to two officers with orders to sail to Spain aboard the best ship in the fleet. They were to contact Martin Cortes de Monroy and, together with him, appeal to the king. It was a gamble, but Cortes was used to gambling, and winning.

After the messengers put to sea, Cortes bribed the sailing masters of the remaining vessels to spread the rumor that the ships were being destroyed by sea worms. Anything useful—sails, anchors, rigging, tar, ironwork—was salvaged and the ships sunk. Cortes had deliberately cut his line of retreat back to Cuba. The army was now on its own. Soldiers might grumble at the hardships that lay ahead, but he knew they'd have to obey his orders or die in a strange land. There could be no turning back. Like the Totonacs, he had his own army in the palm of his hand.

⌒ ⌒ ⌒

On August 16, 1519, Don Hernan Cortes mustered his army outside Cempoala. About four hundred Spaniards stood at attention or sat on horseback under the blazing sun. Another hundred were to remain with Sandoval to guard Villa Rica and bring news from the coast; these were joined by about seventy-five sailors from the sunken ships. Forty Totonac guides and two hundred porters waited nearby.

Cortes rode past his troops, his eyes moving from face to face. Satisfied, he raised the banner with the golden Cross and pointed to the distant mountains. Then, with Doña Marina walking beside her captain's horse, the army began to move. A shout exploded from the ranks, making the air ring.

"To Mexico! To Mexico!"

3 The March to Mexico

●◎●

A journey of two hundred fifty miles lay between the shacks of Villa Rica de la Vera Cruz and the temples of Tenochtitlan. Cortes's Totonac guides had mapped a route that would take them through the territories of peoples who hated the Aztecs. If everything went well, the Spaniards could count on a steady flow of supplies, probably even fighting men, from these peoples.

The *Conquistadores* needed every man they could get. During the early stages of the march, nature treated them as harshly as any human enemy. Their route led from the sweltering beaches and swamps of the hot lands through a belt of cool pine forests and lush valleys at four thousand feet above sea level. From there the path went nearly straight up, through ten-thousand-foot mountain passes lashed by freezing rains.

The months in the tropics began to take their toll. The men were weak, nearly all suffering the chills and fever of malaria. Many endured the retchings of *"vomitio,"* in which anything eaten was thrown up flecked with blood.

93

Cortes himself ran a high fever for days at a time, his eyes, red as coals, contrasting with the pasty-gray of his complexion.

Eventually they reached the land of the Tlaxcalans (Tlash-ca'-lans), a tribe of fierce mountaineer-warriors. Tlaxcala was a lonely island surrounded by Aztec territory. Its people had been fighting their neighbors constantly for nearly a century. Try as they might, the Aztecs were never able to overrun the Tlaxcalans or stay long in their country.

Although unconquered, the Tlaxcalans paid a high price for independence. The Aztecs blockaded their valleys, sealing them off from the outside world. Salt, boiled out of sea water, was unobtainable, as were cotton cloth and colorful bird feathers, so necessary to Indian costumes.

The Tlaxcalans lived and thought like a people under siege: always armed, always alert, always expecting the worst, never trusting anyone. The strangers might or might not be friends. The only way to find out was to test them in battle. A defeat for the strangers would prove that they were unworthy as allies. But if the Tlaxcalans lost, they'd apologize for their error and ask for friendship. They couldn't afford to waste their friendship on people who would be of no help in a war.

One day the Spaniards found a cord tied across the trail. From the cord hung brightly colored pieces of paper cut into strange shapes. Their Totonac guides recoiled in terror, for these were magical charms to cast evil spells on intruders. Cortes, however, didn't scare easily. He cut down the barrier and sent four Indians to tell the Tlaxcalans that he came in peace.

They didn't believe him. No sooner did the army cross the border, than it was forced to fight a series of skirmishes. The Spaniards were not gods to the Tlaxcalans, nor did they panic at the sight of horses. Warriors ran up to the charging animals and tried to topple their riders from the saddle.

One warrior lopped off a horse's head with a single blow of his sword-club.

After the last skirmish, Xicotenga, the Tlaxcalan war chief, sent Cortes hundreds of turkeys and baskets of tortillas. He wasn't being generous to a brave enemy, for with the food came a message: let the strangers put fat on their skinny bodies, because the Tlaxcalans meant to make a tasty meal of them. Already women were boiling tomatoes and red chili peppers in their biggest kettles.

The Spaniards faced an army of fifty thousand—five divisions of ten thousand men, each with its own commander. They spent the night before the battle on their knees praying and confessing their sins to Padre Olmedo, the expedition's priest. At sunup everyone able to walk, including the wounded in their bandages, took up a weapon and went out to meet the enemy.

Hour after hour, the armies tore at each other. The Indians were so tightly packed that every shot and jab found a mark. Without counting their losses, the Tlaxcalans stepped over their dead, closed ranks, and kept coming. "How they began to charge us!" Bernal Diaz recalled. "What a hail of stones fell from their slings! As for their bowmen, their arrows lay like corn on the threshing floor. . . . The men with swords and shields and . . . lances, how they pressed on us and with what valor and what mighty shouts and yells they charged upon us!"

Luckily for the Spaniards, the enemy wasn't able to bring his full power to bear at once. The Tlaxcalan commanders disliked one another so much that they wouldn't cooperate. Calls for reinforcements by hard-pressed chiefs went unanswered, allowing the *Conquistadores* to push them back until they broke off the battle.

It had been a close shave and Cortes wasn't pleased. For the first time anywhere in the New World, a Spanish army had been checked by Indians. True, he wasn't defeated, but neither had he won. And winning was the whole game to Cortes. Another "tie" like this might ruin his army altogether.

While his troops were nursing their wounds, Cortes sent another peace offer. This time the Tlaxcalans took him at his word. Ambassadors visited his camp with food and an invitation to visit their capital, Tlaxcala city.

The march to Mexico. Cortes, seated, listens as Doña Marina translates the greetings of a delegation of Indians. The Indians have brought gifts, corn cakes and tamales for the people, hay for the horses. (Redrawn from the Lienzo de Tlaxcala. "Lienzo" is Spanish for linen; thus the "Linens of Tlaxcala" are paintings on long sheets of linen cloth dealing with the adventures of the men of Tlaxcala.)

The Spaniards were surprised at their reception. It was as if the recent battles had never happened. The people cheered and pelted the soldiers with flowers, welcoming them as old friends. Cortes's offers of friendship, plus the courage of his soldiers, had convinced the Indans that they were worthy friends. They didn't give their friendship easily, but when they did, it was forever. "We will give you all that you desire, Malinche," said Xicotenga, "even ourselves and our children, and we are ready to die for you." The Tlaxcalans became Cortes's firmest allies, generous, intelligent, and as tough as the *Conquistadores* themselves. Several Tlaxcalan nobles became Christians and gave their daughters as brides to Spanish officers.

Best of all, they told everything they knew about the Aztecs. Men who had visited Tenochtitlan as ambassadors or spies drew pictures of the city's layout, the causeways, the bridges, the canals. They also showed large paintings on cloth of battles with the Aztecs, illustrating their weapons and fighting style. Before long, Cortes had formed a clear picture in his mind of his future enemies and the task before him.

When Montezuma learned of the "god's" alliance with his enemies, he sent more gifts and word that he'd pay any tribute so long as he stayed away from Tenochtitlan. Cortes had only to name his price and the Chief Speaker would gladly pay. Cortes accepted the gifts with many thanks, but refused to turn back. When he left Tlaxcala, in September 1519, a thousand of Xicotenga's best warriors formed his rear guard. The chief had offered ten times that number, but Cortes refused. He didn't want to show too much force, or frighten Montezuma needlessly.

Day by day the army advanced toward its destination. It seemed more like a victory parade than an invasion. Towns that had seemed loyal to the Aztecs for centuries opened their gates and received the *Conquistadores* with rejoicing as liberators. Only one place resisted, and it paid a fearful penalty.

Cholula (Cho-lo'o-la), a city of twenty thousand houses and as many temples as there are days in the year, was only a two-day march from Tlaxcala. As the column approached, it was met by a delegation of nobles who offered Cortes the hospitality of their city. The Tlaxcalans, however, had to camp in a field outside; the two peoples had often fought, and the Cholulans wanted to keep them at a safe distance.

The Spaniards were given quarters in a large building with a walled courtyard, next to a temple. As they'd come to expect, Indians brought them huge amounts of food and flowers for their enjoyment.

Suddenly, after four days of hospitality, things changed. There was less food, and that of poor quality. When soldiers tried to approach people, they kept their distance and grinned as if they knew about some secret joke. Totonac scouts, who'd been allowed to stay with Cortes, reported that the city was being prepared for a battle. Barricades had been built in the side streets, blocking the avenues of retreat. Holes were dug in the main streets, filled with sharpened stakes, and covered with brush to trap the horses. Small children had been sacrificed to the war god. Most disturbing of all, an Aztec army was camped out of sight nearby, behind a range of hills.

It is difficult to say why Montezuma sent this army, when until now he hadn't tried anything stronger than bribes and magic to turn back the strangers. Perhaps he was using the Cholulans as puppets to test the Spaniards once again. If the Cholulans were defeated, that would be final proof that the strangers were divine. Montezuma would then tell Cortes that they had acted on their own, against his orders. But if they seemed to be winning, that would prove that the strangers were human and the Aztec army could rush in to wipe them out. We'll never know what Montezuma's reasons were. What is sure is that the Spaniards were being set up for a surprise attack.

Doña Marina discovered proof of the plot. The wife of a Cholulan leader who admired her beauty and wanted her to marry her son gave away the scheme. She warned Doña Marina to leave the Spanish quarters and come to her house, for the attack would come when Cortes least expected. If any Spaniards should be taken alive, they'd be dragged by the hair to the top of a pyramid and sacrificed. Cortes, the fallen "god," would be sent to Tenochtitlan for special treatment.

Doña Marina went straight to her captain with the story. Immediately he arrested a priest and had him tortured into confessing the plot and that it was Montezuma's idea.

Next morning, two thousand Cholulan "porters" streamed into the courtyard to prepare for the march. Healthy, high-spirited young men, they exchanged knowing glances, unmindful of the armor-clad Spaniards at the gates and along the walls.

While they waited, Cortes called thirty of Cholula's leading men into his room. He came right to the point, describing their whole plot. The men gasped in amazement, for Cortes obviously had supernatural mind-reading powers. He then announced the penalty for their treachery: death.

That announcement was the signal for a musketeer to fire his weapon. Suddenly the huge wooden doors to the courtyard slammed shut. There was a loud, metallic swishing as swords were drawn from their scabbards.

It was a massacre. For three hours the *Conquistadores* stabbed, hacked, clubbed, and shot the trapped Indians until none remained alive. Blood in some places in the courtyard was ankle-deep. The Tlaxcalans, hearing the commotion, charged into the city killing hundreds more.

Cholula was looted, its temples burned, and their idols sent crashing in pieces down the pyramids' steps. Hundreds of priests were driven up the main pyramid and thrown to their deaths. A great wooden cross was placed atop the pyramid to symbolize the power of the *Conquistadores'* God. The Tlaxcalans were so impressed by their allies that from then on they used the war cry *"Santiago!"*

Horrible as it was, the Cholula massacre was not simply an exercise in brutality. Cortes's brutality was never for its own sake, his violence never without a well thought-out purpose. Cholula was meant to be a lesson for others, a warning of the punishment certain to follow if they dared even think of treachery. As for Montezuma, who was really to blame, Cortes resolved to deal with him later. Until then, he'd keep up the pretense of friendship and goodwill.

∾   ∾   ∾

The invaders marched out of Cholula, heading for the mountain pass that opened into the Valley of Mexico. Aztecs who saw them along the way carried the memory for the rest of their lives. Dogs came with the vanguard, in the lead. The ferocious animals strained at their leashes, baring long yellow teeth.

Soldiers followed in battle formation, rank upon rank, their boots stirring up whirlpools of dust. Spear points and halberd blades glistened; pennants fluttered. Armor and swords clashed and clanged with each step.

Behind them came the cavalry, tiny bells jingling on bridles. The horses winnied and neighed, their hooves clattering. Sweat rolled down their sides, making their flanks slick and shiny. The Tlaxcalans covered the rear of the column, their feather banners swaying with the rhythm of the march.

After Cholula, Montezuma gave up any hopes of turning back the strangers. He called a council of his greatest

The Cholula massacre as seen by an Indian artist. The Spaniards and their Tlaxcalan allies, armed with sword-clubs, charge up a pyramid to come to grips with their enemies. Doña Marina, who revealed the plot to Cortes, stands at the right, pointing to the scene of the butchery. (Picture redrawn from the Lienzo de Tlascala.)

lords to tell them of his decision. The lords were solemn as
the Chief Speaker said the strangers were definitely divine.
Since they had overcome every obstacle put in their way,
they'd have to be welcomed, whatever the consequences.

Not everyone believed that the Quetzelcoatl legend
was coming true. Cuitlahuac (Quit-la-hu'ac), Montezuma's
younger brother, pleaded for all-out war before it was too
late. "I pray to our gods that you will not do this thing.
The strangers will cast you out of your own house and
overthrow your throne, and you will not recover either!"
The whole council nodded in agreement, although no one
else spoke for fear of provoking their Angry Young Lord.
Montezuma then sent ambassadors to guide the strangers
into the center of the Aztec world.

To reach Tenochtitlan, Cortes had to cross a twelve-
thousand-foot pass between the volcanoes Popocatapetl
and Iztaccihuatl. Popocatapetl had become active recently,
sending columns of smoke and ash thousands of feet into
the sky. The Spaniards believed its rumbling was a sign of
God's favor.

On reaching the top of the pass, they glimpsed the
Valley of Mexico for the first time. It lay in the distance,
spread out before them like a gigantic map. The Lake of
the Moon caught the sun's rays, shining silvery-blue in the
clear air. The causeways appeared as fine threads linking
the island with the cities along the shore. Even at a distance
of forty miles Tenochtitlan's temples sparkled.

From here on, the route went steadily downhill. The
army marched for three days, halting each night at camps
prepared by the Aztecs for their comfort. By evening of
the fourth day, it was at Iztapalapan (Is-ta-pala-pan) on
the causeway leading to the capital from the southwest.
The city's white temples, clearly visible five miles away,
reminded the Spaniards of fairy cities in their own legends.
Some soldiers kept asking whether the things they saw
were real and if they weren't dreaming.

The Spaniards as the Indians saw them. Cortes and his army pass the giant volcanoes southeast of Tenochtitlan on their way to the capital. Popocatepetl, on the right, is belching smoke, which the Spaniards interpreted as a sign of God's favor. (Redrawn from Codex Florentino.)

On the morning of November 15, 1519, the army set out on the last leg of its journey. As it marched along the causeway, Aztecs by the tens of thousands streamed out of the capital. Canoes lined both sides of the causeway, packed so tightly together that you could have walked from one to another. The causeway itself was lined with onlookers, leaving only a narrow corridor for the marchers to pass through.

The *Conquistadores* were nervous; they remembered the treachery at Cholula and the warnings of their allies that the Aztecs could never be trusted. But there was no danger—this time. The people's faces beamed with wonder and respect.

Time and again the column halted to receive the greeting of local chiefs dressed in their finery. Each kneeled in turn before Cortes, touched the earth, and kissed his fingers as a sign of respect.

As the column neared the city, it was met by the advancing royal procession of nobles decked out in swaying featherwork and flashing jewelry. The leaders carried bunches of flowers and marched in silence in honor of the one who was following. Barefooted, eyes cast down, they swept the ground with straw brooms and spread colorful cotton mats to cushion his feet from the earth. Musicians set the pace with eerie rhythms played on drums, cymbals, whistles, flutes, and rattles. In their midst came a litter carried on the shoulders of four nobles. It had a canopy of green quetzel feathers streaked with golden thread and strands of white pearls.

The procession stopped and the litter was gently lowered in front of Cortes. There emerged a tall, thin man in his early forties. His eyes were dark, his face serious; a few thin whiskers grew on his chin and at the corners of his mouth. The Spaniards couldn't help noticing that his sandals were made of leopard skin with soles of solid gold.

Cortes swung out of the saddle and stood before the Aztec ruler with Doña Marina at his side. He stared straight into his face, which shocked the nobles, who'd been trained from childhood to avert their eyes from his sacred being. Without speaking, the two men exchanged gifts. Cortes gave a necklace of glass beads strung on a golden cord and received a collar hung with eight life-size shrimps of pure gold.

"Is it you? Is it really you? Are you truly Montezuma?" he asked.

"I am he," replied the Aztec, bowing. That bow left no doubt about who would be master. Straightening himself, Montezuma welcomed Cortes as the god Quetzelcoatl.

"O Lord, our Lord," he said, "you have arrived in this land, your land, your own city of Mexico, to take posession of your throne."

When he finished, Cortes whispered to Doña Marina, "Tell Montezuma we are his friends. There is nothing to fear. . . . Tell him we love him well and that our hearts are contented. We have come to his house as friends. There is nothing to fear."

In fact, the Angry Young Lord had everything to fear from his guests.

✿   ✿   ✿

Montezuma escorted the Spaniards to a palace that had belonged to his late father, Chief Speaker Axayacatl (Ashay-a'h-catl), Lord Water Monster. The palace was located outside the Serpent Wall, in the shadow of the great pyramid. Its halls, courtyards, and corridors easily housed the Spanish army. Its scores of spotlessly clean rooms had polished floors of scented wood and walls hung with brilliantly colored tapestries. None of the strangers, including Cortes, had ever seen such a luxurious building. Their Tlaxcalan allies, however, weren't offered rooms, but made to camp in the open courtyard; the Aztecs hated them as savages fit only for sacrifice.

Crowds continued to mill about the palace gates long after Montezuma returned to his own quarters. Their fascination with the strangers turned to terror when Cortes test-fired a couple of cannon to see how they'd react. As expected, the noise and smoke sent them scurrying in every direction. Cortes then set up his cannon to cover the entrances, posted guards, and ordered the men to bed down.

The exhausted soldiers found little rest during their first night in Tenochtitlan. Everything was so new, so strange, so menacing. They were in the center of a vast fortress-city, inhabited by a famous warrior people. They had noticed that the causeways were cut by canals, and that the bridges over these canals could be easily removed, trapping them. From the courtyard of their palace they had a clear view of the sacrificial stone in front of Hummingbird Wizard's temple. Priests marked the nighttime hours with blasts on conch-shell trumpets. The strangers from the sunrise had plenty to think about as they tossed restlessly on their sleeping mats.

The next day Cortes and his captains visited Montezuma in his palace on the other side of the square. The building was similar to their own quarters, only larger and more elegant. Montezuma lived as well as the grandest European prince. His palace was a small, self-contained city with thousands of inhabitants. Its hundreds of rooms were grouped around three courtyards, each the size of a parade ground. The floors and halls were of polished marble and jasper; the woodwork, neatly joined without nails, gave off the cool scent of the forest. All was quiet, except for the patter of servants' bare feet and the splashing of fountains in the courtyards.

Montezuma lived with his two official wives and hundreds of other women, mostly chiefs' daughters given by their fathers as gifts, on the second floor. The first floor was occupied by the fabled "halls of Montezuma," vast rooms used by the law courts, the treasury, and for public ceremonies. The palace was so large that one of Cortes's men returned to it again and again out of curiosity, without being able to see it all. Its corridors seemed to stretch on forever. An army of three thousand guards and servants kept things running smoothly.

The palace cooks were among the most valued servants. Montezuma was fed with the same care as they'd devote to a god. For each meal they prepared at least thirty different dishes for him to choose from—turkey, quail, duck, goose, wild pig, venison, fruits and vegetables. Fish, shrimp, and sea turtles, which had been swimming in the Gulf of Mexico the day before, were brought across the mountains on the backs of porters. Sometimes, to make doubly sure that the fish stayed fresh, they were carried alive in tanks of sea water.

Montezuma ate in private, shielded from view by a golden screen. When he finished, the screen was removed and women brought his favorite treat, golden cups filled with a foaming brown liquid. *Chocolatl*, from which we get the word "chocolate," was made from crushed cacao nuts boiled in water. Honey, vanilla, and spices were added to the liquid, which was then whipped into a froth. Montezuma drank dozens of cups of *chocolatl* each day.

If he was in the mood, the court dwarfs and hunchbacks were called to entertain with slapstick skits and juggling tricks. These people, and others with birth defects, lived in the palace and were treated with respect until an eclipse of the sun. When the moon passed in front of Huitzilopochtil's chariot, blotting it from view, priests gave them messages to repeat to the god and then cut out their hearts.

As Montezuma watched the performance, he puffed gold-covered pipes filled with *tabaco* leaves. Tobacco, unknown in Europe until Columbus brought some back from his first voyage, was smoked by most American Indian tribes for pleasure and because they believed the gods enjoyed the aroma of its smoke.

Botanical gardens, aviaries, and a zoo stood near the royal palace. Montezuma's gardens were larger and more beautiful than any in Europe at this time. His servants scoured the empire, gathering the most interesting shrubs, trees, and flowers. Flower beds, tended by three hundred gardeners, covered many acres and were crisscrossed by tree-shaded paths.

Covered aviaries housed birds of every description, few of which the Spaniards had ever seen. Ducks and geese had their own keepers and were fed on the same fish they ate in the wild. Huge cages held birds of prey: hawks, eagles, falcons, vultures. Each day keepers fed them five hundred turkeys. Their feathers were plucked from time to time and sent to Montezuma's artists to weave into headdresses and wall decorations.

The Spaniards, who had never seen a zoo in Europe, for they didn't exist at this time, found Montezuma's both fascinating and frightening. Crocodiles lolled in pools, covered with mud, their horny hides resembling fallen tree trunks. Boa constrictors with midsections bulging with pigs swallowed whole draped themselves on shaded branches. Poisonous snakes were kept in earthenware jars; and it is here that Europeans first made the acquaintance of snakes with tails that rattled like dry seeds in a gourd. Larger animals—jaguars, mountain lions, wolves, coyotes, foxes—were kept in separate cages. Keepers tossed the meat eaters the bodies of people killed in sacrifice.

Cortes took in the sights, not as a curious tourist, but as a general studying an objective. His welcome, he knew, was bound to wear off. Sooner or later some incident would touch off a war. Before that happened, he had to have a clear picture of the battleground. A week after his arrival, he asked Montezuma for a guided tour of Tenochtitlan. The Chief Speaker agreed, for he was proud of his city; besides, in his mind it already belonged to his divine guest.

Aztec noblemen led the way as the whole Spanish army paraded out of its quarters. The soldiers were as curious about the Indians as they were about them. The first stop on the tour was the market of Tlatelolco in the northern part of the city. The Spaniards were startled by its size and the orderliness of the thousands who came there to do business. The market square was twice as large as Salamanca's, one of the largest in Europe. Covered arcades surrounded it to protect the people from the weather and to give the various tradespeople space to show off their goods. Food was heaped in piles on straw mats or hung from crossbeams: vegetables, fruits, maize, poultry, honey, tamales, cooked and fresh meat, young dogs for eating. Luxuries such as cocoa beans and tobacco were offered for sale. Passersby stopped to watch skilled craftsmen cut precious stones, carve religious statues, and make golden jewelry. Gold dust was sold in clear goose quills or offered as nuggets. Slaves, their necks fastened to long poles by heavy collars, waited their turn on the auction block. Cloth, thread, dyes, pottery, lumber, adobe bricks, sandals, medicines—anything anyone might ever need could be bought at a set price or after a little bargaining.

Police stood on raised platforms, keeping an eye on the crowds. Nearby, in the shade, the judges held court. They were strict, and their decisions final. The goods of dishonest merchants were destroyed; thieves were strangled.

Leaving the market, the Spaniards retraced their steps to the great pyramid. There Cortes, his captains, and a few picked soldiers were met by husky priests who offered to carry them up the steps. Cortes took one look at these black-clothed men with bloodclotted hair and started up the hundred and fourteen steps by himself, his men following close behind.

He found Montezuma waiting for him at the top. The Chief Speaker had gone ahead to sacrifice some boys, to keep the gods in a good mood. Seeing Cortes flushed and breathless, he said that he should have allowed the priests to carry him. Cortes stood up straight, squared his shoulders, and replied that Spaniards never tired of anything.

Taking Cortes by the hand, Montezuma led him to the edge of the platform and pointed out everything of interest. Cortes had a birdseye view of the approaches to the city, the causeways, the main streets, the canals, and the aqueduct from Chapultepec. He studied the features carefully, fixing them in his mind for future reference.

Cortes, smiling, now asked Montezuma for an unexpected favor: to see the shrine of Huitzilopochtli. Montezuma hesitated, then, after a hurried conference with the temple priests, invited the Spaniards into the holiest place in the Aztec world.

The house of Hummingbird Wizard was dark, except for light reflecting off the polished flagstones outside. Shadows flickered across the walls. Priests danced around the visitors waving long-handled bowls with burning incense.

Squinting into the darkened chamber, the Spaniards saw the gigantic idol of Huitzilopochtli. These men were battle-hardened veterans used to seeing terrible sights. But Huitzilopochtli made them step back in horror. He was an image out of a nightmare. All the fears of the Aztec people, their dread of the all-powerful forces of nature that could crush them in an instant, seemed to radiate from that statue.

Bernal Diaz remembered the scene fifty years later. Although he had become blind, every detail appeared to him as vividly as on the first day. "It had a very broad face and monstrous and terrible eyes, and the whole of his body was covered with precious stones, and gold and pearls, and with seed pearls stuck on with a paste that they make in this country with a sort of root, and all the body and head were covered with it, and the body was girdled with great

snakes made of gold and precious stones, and in one hand
he held a bow and in the other some arrows. . . . Huichilobos* had round his neck some Indians' faces and other
things like hearts of Indians, the former made of gold and
the latter of silver, with many precious blue stones. There
were some braziers with incense which they call copal,
and in them they were burning the hearts of three of the
Indians whom they had sacrificed that day. . . . All the
walls of the oratory were so splashed and encrusted with
blood that they were black, the floor was the same and the
whole place stank vilely. . . . The walls were so clotted
with blood and the soil so bathed with it that in the
slaughterhouses of Spain there is not such another stench.
Everything was so clotted with blood, and there was so
much of it, that I curse the whole of it, and as it stank like
a slaughterhouse we hastened to clear out of such a bad
stench and worse sight."

Outside, in the fresh air, Cortes told Montezuma how
he felt about what they'd seen. Speaking through Doña
Marina, he told "Señor Montezuma" that he couldn't understand how such a wise prince could believe such evil
things were gods. "They are devils," he said, adding that it
would be best if the Aztecs allowed him to set up a cross
and a statue of the Virgin Mary in one of the temples.

Montezuma was stunned. The priests began to mutter
among themselves. They could hardly believe their ears.
The nerve of him! The insolence! What an insult to want
to put a woman's image near that of the war god! Swallow-
ing his anger, the Chief Speaker told Cortes that he would
never have shown him the temple had he suspected such
rudeness. "Malinche," he said, "we consider (our gods) to
be very good, for they give us health and rains and good
seed times and seasons and as many victories as we desire,

* The Spaniards had trouble pronouncing the name Huitzilopochtli.
Instead they called him Huichilobos, which means "Witchy-wolf."

and I pray you not to say another word to their dishonor."
The gods were already angry enough, and would have to
be calmed with more sacrifices.

After climbing down the pyramid, the Spaniards saw
more horrors on the way through the great square. They
passed rooms with large knives and chopping blocks, where
sacrificial victims' bodies were prepared for feasts or the
zoo. They also saw skull racks containing, they believed,
over one hundred twenty-five thousand skulls. Shaken and
fearful, they returned to their quarters, having seen enough
for one day.

～   ～   ～

The temple visit was a turning point for both sides.
Montezuma and the priests began to see Cortes as evil.
God or no god, he'd insulted Huitzilopochtli and offended
their deepest religious beliefs. One day, if he went too far,
he'd have to be resisted.

Cortes, too, made an important decision. He knew that
Montezuma had only to snap his fingers for warriors to fill
the streets of Tenochtitlan. But his keen eye also detected
the Aztecs' greatest weakness. He noticed that the people
had been trained from childhood to obey their superiors,
not to think for themselves. That obedience was the source
of the tribe's unity. Yet without their Chief Speaker, the
Aztecs would become a mob, a body without a brain, in-
capable of action. To save themselves, the Spaniards decided
to kidnap their host and hold him as their "insurance
policy."

Cortes knew the plan was dangerous, but so was sitting
by and doing nothing. To avoid suspicion, he'd have to go
to Montezuma with a handful of men. They'd have to
seize a powerful ruler in his own well-guarded palace in
the center of a city filled with warriors. One slip-up and
their hearts would wind up in the bowl in front of
Huitzilopochtli's idol.

On the morning of November 14, 1519, nine days after arriving in Tenochtitlan, Cortes led five of his captains and a squad of soldiers to the royal palace. His men were prepared for anything, good or bad, having made their peace with God during a whole night of prayer and confession. The sentries let them pass, although they were armed to the teeth. They were used to seeing Spaniards wearing armor and carrying weapons; indeed, it was known that they slept in their armor, their swords near their hands.

The little party was shown into the reception room, where they found Montezuma as courteous as ever. He asked about Cortes's health and had gifts brought for the men. Cortes came straight to the point. A Spanish patrol had been ambushed near Villa Rica and some soldiers killed. He didn't believe for a moment that Montezuma had anything to do with the attack, he said. But it would be a gesture of good will if he came to live with his guests in Lord Water Monster's palace. He'd be shown every kindness, for, he knew, the Spaniards loved him. Everything would be as before, except that he'd be among friends.

Montezuma refused even to listen to this demand. He was a mighty ruler and no one spoke to him this way. Besides, his nobles would never allow him to be taken away.

Cortes insisted, politely.

Montezuma began to waver. He offered his three favorite children as hostages in his place. He even burst into tears at the indignity.

Cortes was unmoved. He could have had Montezuma dragged away in chains, but that would have started a war, something he hoped to avoid. He wanted the Aztec ruler to tell his servants that he was going of his own free will.

Hours passed in aimless argument. The Spaniards began to lose patience. Finally an officer burst out: "What's the use of talking? Either we take him or we knife him. If we don't, we're dead men." Doña Marina translated his words, adding that the Spaniards would kill him if he didn't go immediately and without a fuss. There was nothing more to discuss.

Montezuma gave in. He called for his litter, declaring that he wanted to stay with his friends for a while. Palace officials couldn't believe their ears. Something must be wrong, they thought, but they were powerless to interfere without a royal command. Barefooted, with eyes lowered, they brought the litter and helped him inside. Some wept openly. Cortes and his men became all smiles and soft words, patting him on the back for being so "reasonable." It was a kidnapping pure and simple.

Word of the move swept the city. Shocked people jammed the streets, surging around the litter and its screen of Spanish guards. Montezuma's command opened a path through the throng, only to have it reform outside Lord Water Monster's palace. Again Cortes had a cannon fired. And again the Aztecs fled in panic.

As soon as Montezuma saw the expressions on the sentries' faces, he knew he was really a prisoner. Perhaps he also knew that he'd never again be free, and that the people, deprived of his leadership, would never rescue him.

Few captives have ever lived as well as Montezuma. His entire court—wives, cooks, jesters, servants, officials—came with him to his new quarters. During the following weeks a strange friendship developed between prisoner and jailers. Spanish soldiers took off their helmets and bowed whenever they saw him. He grew to like them, and they him, especially his generosity. He was freer with gifts than anyone they'd ever known. Cortes *spoke* grandly about making them rich, but Montezuma *gave* them gold jewelry, fine cloth, and maidservants for the slightest favor. Once, when a soldier behaved rudely, Cortes ordered him hung. Only Montezuma's plea for mercy saved the man's life, which pleased his fellow soldiers no end.

Captivity broke Montezuma's spirit. The Angry Young Lord became a weak, meek shadow of himself. Captive and jailer had a simple arrangement: Montezuma ruled the Aztec empire and Cortes ruled Montezuma. He did everything the "god" ordered, except give up faith in Huitzilopochtli. During a ceremony in the main hall of Lord Water Monster's palace, he surrendered the empire to Cortes, and through him to King Charles of Spain. The ceremony was sad, his sobs so heartbreaking that even the hardbitten soldiers wept.

Yet their sympathy never interfered with their greed for gold. Montezuma was their key to unlocking the riches of the Aztecs. With him in their hands, there was nothing to prevent them from going on a looting spree.

Teams of Spanish soldiers and Aztec guides visited the farthest corners of the empire to map gold and silver deposits Indians had mined for centuries. The ruler himself led Cortes to the capital's treasures. They went first to the Teocalco, the public treasure house. The building was crammed with precious goods of every kind: golden fans set with jewels and quetzel feathers, ankle rings with golden bells, golden necklaces, bracelets and arm bands, gold and silver shields. Then they followed Montezuma to his personal treasurehouse in the zoo, where they found precious things heaped almost to the ceiling.

The sight of so much wealth drove the Spaniards wild. They ran around the rooms, not knowing what to grab first. Indians who saw them remembered the scenes for future generations. "The Spaniards," they told Father Bernardino de Sahagun, "grinned like little beasts and pounded each other with delight. When they entered the hall of treasures, it was as if they had arrived in Paradise. They searched everywhere and coveted everything. They were slaves to their greed. They seized these treasures as if they were their own, and as if this plunder had come to them by good luck."

Art of the featherworker. This ceremonial shield, made entirely of feathers, shows a blue coyote, symbol of war, singing a war song against an orange background. One of the few surviving examples of Aztec handicrafts.

Delicate works of art were torn apart for their precious metals. Feathers, useless to the Spaniards, were left for the Tlaxcalans, who valued them more than gold. The leftovers—statues, carvings, pottery, illustrated books—were burned. Only one piece of featherwork survived. It is the ceremonial shield of Lord Water Monster and it shows a coyote singing a war song. You can see this shield today in the Museum of Folk Art in Vienna, Austria.

After the looting of the treasure house in the zoo, Doña Marina climbed to the roof and shouted to the nobles in the courtyard below: "O Mexicans, come here! The Spaniards are tired. Bring food and fresh water. Why don't you come? Are you angry?" They were both angry and frightened, but didn't dare act on their own. They set food and drink on the ground and ran away.

The Spanish quarters overflowed with gold. Aztec goldsmiths were hustled in at swordpoint and forced to melt down the treasure to make it easier to carry. The "King's fifth," or royal share, was formed into bars and marked with his coat of arms. Cortes also took a fifth; he felt entitled to so much because he'd paid most of the expedition's expenses out of his own pocket. A portion was shared out among the men, who had it made into heavy chains to be worn around the neck. The captains, most of whom were already landowners in Cuba, put aside their gold to buy more property or allow them to live as gentlemen in Spain. The common soldiers, who owned only their weapons and the clothes on their backs, thought only of the present. They gambled away their shares on a toss of the dice or with playing cards made from drum skins. There was no end to the treasure, they felt. There'd always be another Aztec treasure house to loot.

➢   ➢   ➢

Beginning with the landing at Cozumel, Cortes had lectured the Indians about his religion. In one town after another— Tabasco, Cempoala, Cholula, and those in between—he had tumbled the idols from the temples, replacing them with crosses and statues of the Virgin Mary holding the baby Jesus. Only the Tlaxcalans were left alone, because he needed them too badly as allies.

The sight of Huitzilopochtli made him more determined than ever to rid Mexico of paganism. Now, with Montezuma his captive, he decided to act. One day in April, 1520, Cortes and ten men bounded up the steps of the great pyramid. Upon reaching the top, they found a rope curtain hung with bells pulled across the doorway of Hummingbird Wizard's temple; the device was an alarm to warn the priests of intruders. A few sword strokes brought the curtain down, setting off a jangling racket that brought the priests running.

The Spaniards stormed into the temple, only to find another curtain blocking the way. Again slashing steel cleared the way. The moment the curtain fell, they found themselves face to face with Huitzilopochtli, who sat glaring at them from behind a golden mask.

According to eyewitness accounts, Cortes's face reddened. The veins in his neck bulged. His anger exploded. "O God," he shouted, "why do You allow the devil to be so honored in this land?" Snatching an iron crowbar from a soldier, he leaped into the air and struck the idol in the face, knocking away the mask. The priests, outraged at the insult, sent for help. Cortes ordered a soldier to bring reinforcements.

A few more words and a few more minutes would have had Aztecs and Spaniards at each other's throats. War was averted only because Montezuma arrived in time, under guard. A glance told him what had happened. To prevent war, he suggested a compromise: Let the Virgin Mary's statue be placed outside the temple, on the pyramid platform.

Cortes, however, had gone too far to compromise. He was a champion of the "True God," he believed. Let the priests fetch water and scrub the bloodstained walls clean. Let them get the idol out of sight, or he'd have his men do it for them. "I shall take great pleasure in fighting for my God against yours, which are no gods at all," he thundered.

Once again Montezuma backed down. A few days later, workers and priests mounted the pyramid in a solemn procession. Carefully, using a system of ropes and levers, they began to lower the idols of Huitzilopochtli and Tlaloc. They worked in total silence, without uttering a word; the only sound was the creaking of rope and the scraping of stone on wood. When the idols were taken away, Cortes had their temples scrubbed clean and whitewashed with lime water. He then led the troops up the side of the pyramid to hear Padre Olmedo say mass.

The Aztecs neither forgot nor forgave the incident. One day a couple of weeks later, Montezuma asked to see Cortes in his private rooms. This time the Aztec felt that he had the upper hand. He told Cortes that the leading priests had shut themselves up in another temple to seek the gods' advice. After days of fasting, drug-taking and offering their blood, the gods spoke to them in their dreams. The Spaniards were evil, they said, and had to be destroyed. If the Aztecs disobeyed this command, the gods would unleash the forces of nature against them. In a flash, the Fifth Sun would come to an end. Montezuma believed that the only way to avoid disaster was for the Spaniards to leave Tenochtitlan as quickly as possible. Let them take their treasure and go while they could.

Cortes was not surprised; he had been expecting something of the sort for a long time. The Chief Speaker's warning, he thought to himself, came in the nick of time. It would allow him to strengthen his defenses and, if necessary, massacre his opponents. Smiling broadly, he replied that he'd gladly leave, except he had no ships in which to sail away.

Montezuma also smiled. His friend, he said, unrolling a cloth scroll, needn't worry about ships. For on the scroll were drawings of other Spaniards, many of them, with ships, horses, and cannon. They had just landed in the territory of the Totonacs.

Those pictures hit Cortes with the force of a lightning bolt. Struggling to keep his smile, he said he was happy to hear the news, for his friends had come to his aid at last.

～   ～   ～

The newcomers were from Cuba. Governor Velasquez, vowing revenge when Cortes sailed against his orders, had spent a year carefully assembling a force to punish the renegade. The army, the largest Spanish force seen so far in the New World, consisted of nine hundred men with eighty horses and twenty cannon. It sailed in eleven ships under the command of Panfilo de Navarez, a soldier known for his cruelty to prisoners.

As soon as Navarez landed, he was met by Aztec ambassadors who thought him a friend of the "god" visiting Tenochtitlan. They were surprised to hear him call Cortes a traitor. Navarez boasted that when he caught up with Cortes he'd cut his ears off and return him to Cuba in a cage.

The ambassadors' report cheered Montezuma. So the strangers from the sunrise were human after all. And Malinche was merely a man, not the god Quetzelcoatl. At last the Angry Young Lord was stirred to action. He sent Navarez secret messages of welcome, together with golden gifts. Nothing would have pleased him more than to have the strangers turn their fire and thunder against each other.

Navarez, however, wasn't in the same league as Cortes. A greedy man, he was also stupid. Instead of offering to share the gifts, he kept them for himself, angering his men.

Cortes knew nothing of Montezuma's dealings with Navarez, or that Navarez's men felt cheated. What he did know was that his fellow Spaniards loved gold and would do anything to get it. And he had plenty of the yellow metal.

Cortes sent Padre Olmedo to the enemy camp with a sackful of gold and jewels. The priest was to distribute this among Navarez's officers and men, telling them it was only a sample of what they could expect if they joined him. Actually Cortes was a generous, forgiving man who wanted only to enrich his countrymen and serve his king and God. By the time Padre Olmedo left the camp, many soldiers had decided that there were better things to do than risk their necks for that cheapskate Navarez.

In the meantime, Cortes marched from Tenochtitlan with only eighty men. Another hundred and fifty were left behind under Pedro de Alvarado to guard the capital and protect Montezuma. Alvarado's instructions were clear: keep the troops out of sight behind the walls of Lord Water Monster's palace and avoid trouble. Above all, he must not provoke a fight.

Cortes led his force toward Cempoala, where the enemy had set up a fortified camp; Navarez's own head-quarters were in a temple atop a pyramid. On the way, Cortes linked up with Gonzalo de Sandoval and about one hundred fifty men from Villa Rica.

Although outnumbered by better than three to one, Cortes had two "equalizers": boldness and surprise. He knew that Navarez felt safe at Cempoala, for only a lunatic would attack against such odds. Very well, he'd play at being a lunatic.

The tiny army marched along, golden chains bounc-ing on their chests, until they reached the outskirts of Cempoala. After midnight, when the enemy camp was fast asleep, the men crossed a shallow stream. Two sentries noticed the black shapes coming toward them and ran to give the alarm. "To arms, to arms, Cortes is coming!"

He came on their heels with drums beating and trumpets blaring. Within minutes one detachment captured Navarez's artillery, while another went for the corral with the cavalry horses. Many soldiers turned their backs on the battle and walked away with their hands in their pockets. "Son" Sandoval rushed up the pyramid to Navarez's headquarters. In the scuffle that followed, someone struck Navarez in the eye with a pike. That blow knocked the arrogance out of him. "Holy Mary, help me!" he shrieked. "They have killed me and put out my eye!" Cortes's men, hearing the commotion, shouted "Victory! Victory! Victory for Cortes! Navarez is dead!"

Navarez wasn't dead, only wounded and a prisoner. When Cortes came to see him, he said sarcastically, "Congratulations for having captured me, Señor Cortes." The reply came as sharp as a pike thrust: "Señor Navarez, my men and I have done many brave deeds since coming to Mexico—but the least deed I have done in this land is to take you."

Navarez's ships were scuttled and he was forced to walk in chains to Villa Rica. His men, however, were treated as long-lost relatives. Cortes gave them gold and promised more to those who'd join him. One by one the captured officers came forward, knelt, and kissed his hand. The common soldiers cheered their new commander.

It was a stunning victory. In one blow, Cortes had increased his army to one thousand three hundred soldiers, ninety-six horses, and over thirty cannon. If he accomplished so much until now with only four hundred men, surely such a force would put the whole of Mexico into his hands.

4 "Noche Triste" Night of Sadness

◉◎

Hernan Cortes was enjoying the sweetness of victory when two Tlaxcalan messengers burst into camp and threw themselves at his feet. They were breathless, having run almost nonstop from Tenochtitlan. The Aztecs had revolted. The Spanish garrison was bottled up in its palace. Cortes was about to taste the bitterness of defeat, and all because Pedro de Alvarado had panicked.

Alvarado, his deputy commander, was a gallant soldier. A year younger than Cortes, he was fair skinned, with blond hair. He was so handsome that the Aztecs called him Tonatiuh, "Child of the Sun." Yet he was changeable as the wind. A jolly man, quick to laugh, he was also deeply suspicious and had a whiplash temper. His hand was never far from a weapon, and he always struck the first blow.

Alvarado would rather have fought alongside his leader than remained in the capital. He understood fighting. It was all so simple, a matter of kill or be killed. He was a soldier, and a good one, not a diplomat. He hadn't an ounce of Cortes's tact and skill at reading others' thoughts. Any

123

responsibility that didn't involve fighting made him nervous.

The Aztecs gave him reason to be jittery. Soon after Cortes left for the coast, Montezuma asked permission to hold the yearly festival of Toxcotl: "Feast of Flowers," in honor of Hummingbird Wizard. Remembering his orders, he approved the request as a gesture of peace.

Preparations for the festival were underway when Alvarado heard disturbing rumors. The Tlaxcalans knew all about Toxcotl and hated everything they knew. For years their finest young men had been sacrificed during its ceremonies. Some Tlaxcalan chiefs came to Alvarado, claiming the Aztecs were using the festival as a cover to gather large numbers of warriors without arousing suspicion. When a priest gave the signal, they'd attack the Spaniards and burn the statue of the Virgin Mary. Huitzilopochtli and Tlaloc would be returned to their temples and their enemies' hearts given as an offering. Tall poles planted in the ground in front of the great pyramid were for the Spaniards' heads, the tallest being reserved for Alvarado.

The story may be true. Alvarado certainly believed it and later explained why on oath to an investigating committee sent by King Charles. We'll never know the whole story. What we can be sure about is that the priests had decided to destroy the Spaniards at the first opportunity. They no longer trusted Montezuma, since anyone who allowed outsiders to expel their gods from their temples was unworthy of leading the Aztec people.

Alvarado was worried. He tried to think what his leader would do. Cortes had already given the answer—at Cholula. The Child of the Sun would put his men on alert and keep sharp lookout. At the first sign of treachery, he'd massacre the Indians.

On the morning of May 16, 1520, thousands of warriors gathered in the square before the great pyramid.

Pedro de Alvarado (1485?–1541) was Cortes's second-in-command and the man responsible for the massacre that triggered the Aztec uprising. After the conquest of Mexico, he went on to conquer and rule Guatemala for Cortes.

Unarmed, they wore their finest feathers and jewelry. The center of attraction was a gigantic image of Hummingbird Wizard made of flower seeds held together with a paste of blood and honey. It was decorated with balls of yellow parrot feathers and eagle down and wrapped in a cape painted with human skulls and hearts. The figure had a harsh expression, even at this time of flowers, and was armed for battle. An arrow-shaped rod of solid gold pierced its nose.

The dancing had already begun when the Spaniards quietly took positions at the gates of the Serpent Wall. Fully armed, they wore steel from head to toe. The visors of their helmets were down, giving them the appearance of faceless creatures from another world. Even so, they were terrified at the scene unfolding before their eyes.

Dancers, hundreds of them, joined hands. Slowly at first, the human chain moved around the towering idol. Eyes half-closed, bodies swaying, they took up the rhythm of the drums. The drums beat louder, faster, sending the dancers into a frantic whirl. Bare feet kicked up miniature dust storms. Sweat poured from their bodies. The women with painted faces and limbs covered with ornaments of red paper watched. Some dancers fell to the ground, kicking and moaning, as if a spirit had become trapped in their bodies and was struggling to break free.

The songs roared, led by priests with lips and cheeks shiny with honey. The tempo quickened, growing more emotional, more threatening. The Indians seemed to be working themselves into a frenzy for something.

The Spanish soldiers exchanged worried glances through their steel visors. Hands gripped weapons tighter. No one seems to have noticed that the dancers were unarmed and that no weapons were in sight. Anyhow, the Child of the Sun, not knowing what to expect, gave the order. Suddenly the gates swung shut, trapping the dancers behind the Serpent Wall.

What happened next is described in the words of the few survivors. Indians by the thousand went down before a whirlwind of gleaming, swinging, steel. "They whose task it was to kill them went only afoot, each with his leather shield, some with their iron-studded shields, and each with iron sword. Then they surrounded those who danced, whereupon they went among the drums. Then they struck the arms of the one who beat the drums; they severed both his hands, and afterwards struck his back so that his neck and head flew off, falling far away. Then they pierced them all with iron lances, and they struck each with the iron swords. Of some they slashed open the back, and then their entrails gushed out. Of some, they split the head; they

The Alvarado massacre. Aztec artists drew this picture of the massacre of dancers in front of the temple of Huitzilopochtli for a book by the Spanish priest and historian, Father Diego Duran.

hacked the heads to pieces; their heads were completely cut up. And of some they hit the shoulder; they split open and cut their bodies to pieces." Those who managed to leap over the wall were skewered by the pikemen waiting on the other side. Only the handful who played dead or crawled under the heaps of bodies survived.

A shock wave of grief spread over Tenochtitlan. Grief gave way to rage. "Oh Mexicans! The chieftains have been put to death, destroyed, shattered!" People shrieked and beat their palms against their mouths. But amid the shrieks were sharp war cries. The Spaniards had gone too far this time.

Drums beat atop the clan temples. Clan storehouses were thrown open. Thousands of men grabbed spears and sword-clubs and bows and arrows and dashed toward the Serpent Wall. They burst in just as the Spaniards were looting the dead. The killers retreated under a storm of missiles.

The enraged people swarmed around Lord Water Monster's palace. Fire-arrows burned part of the building. The food supply was cut off. Luckily, Cortes had dug a well in the courtyard before he left so they at least had water to drink. Yet the Spaniards were trapped.

Alvarado hustled Montezuma up to the roof. Putting a dagger to his throat, he ordered him to calm the crowd— or else!

It didn't work. The people refused to listen to their Chief Speaker. He was greeted with boos and hisses. "Malinche's woman," someone shouted. A hail of arrows drove Alvarado and his hostage indoors.

Montezuma had lost control of his people. His servants were hunted down and killed. Anyone suspected of bringing food to the fortress-palace was knocked on the head and tossed into a canal. Hundreds died at the hands of their own countrymen.

The attacks continued during the following week, until news came of Cortes's victory on the coast. A war council of chiefs decided to let him reenter the capital in order to catch all their enemies in the same net. Suddenly the crowds disappeared from the streets in front of the Spaniards' quarters. An uneasy silence fell over Tenochtitlan.

∾ ∾ ∾

Cortes returned on Sunday, June 24, 1520. He knew he was in trouble the moment he saw the city looming in the distance. The lake, normally teeming with canoes, was empty. No crowds lined the causeway to toss flowers in his path. The city itself seemed a ghost town, hushed and forbidding.

Drawing near the city's center, Cortes fired a cannon. Moments later another cannon boomed in reply. The column then marched double-time to the palace of Lord Water Monster, which they found battle-scarred and reeking of burned wood.

Cortes was in a black mood when he dismounted from his horse. Montezuma and Alvarado were waiting for him in the courtyard, each knowing that things were about to heat up once again. He brushed past the Aztec without a word. He meant to be insulting, for Navarez's officers had told him all about his dealings with their commander.

Cortes's eye caught Alvarado's, beckoning him into a nearby room. "Madman!" he snapped, his eyes burning with rage. The Child of the Sun had undone the work of seven months, bringing the Spaniards to the brink of disaster. Common soldiers had been hung for less.

His temper, however, cooled as quickly as it had erupted. Alvarado was a fool, but he was a fighting fool, and Cortes now needed fighters more than ever. He forgave the captain with a stern warning to be more careful in future.

He also thought again about Montezuma. The Tlatel-olco market had been closed ever since the massacre. His soldiers' rations, already dangerously low, would soon vanish, now that there were so many extra mouths to feed. Cortes send word to his prisoner—"that dog"—that he must have the market opened, or he'd be sorry.

Montezuma proved that he was no coward, only a superstitious man who'd finally seen his error. He replied that he couldn't order food sent while still a captive. If Cortes wanted food, he should send someone the rebels respected. There were plenty of good choices; for after kidnapping Montezuma, the Spaniards had made hostages of several important noblemen, including Cuitlahuac. Why not release him?

Cuitlahuac, whose name means "Keeper of the Kingdom," had wanted to fight the invaders from the beginning, only to be overruled by his brother. Montezuma, now a broken man, realized that the nobles no longer considered him their ruler. He also realized that they wanted to elect someone else in his place. And since Chief Speakers were usually succeeded by their younger brothers, not their sons, Cuitlahuac was next in line.

Cortes, who knew none of this, or of Cuitlahuac's true feelings, took his prisoner's advice. In persuading the Spaniard to release his brother, Montezuma deliberately gave up his throne and guaranteed a war to the death. He willingly sacrificed himself to enable his people to free themselves from their oppressors.

The tribal council met that night to elect the new Chief Speaker. Everything was ready—the warriors, the weapons, the plans. Cuitlahuac took his place at the head of the people.

At dawn, lookouts on the roof of Lord Water Monster's palace heard a strange, distant din. Soon an immense army, a human tidal wave, burst through the streets, flooding the square around the palace.

"Los Indios!" The Indians!

Drummers rapped out the alarm. Soldiers, fully clad in armor, for no one undressed to sleep anymore, ran to their posts.

The battle raged fast and furious. Spears, darts, and stones filled the air. Fire-arrows arched skyward, peaked, and streaked earthward, trailing a banner of flame.

The Spaniards fought like wildmen. Musketeers blazed away, the barrels of their weapons becoming so hot that they burned their hands while taking aim. They couldn't miss, since the Indians were so closely packed that a single bullet might pass through a man's head into that of the man behind—two for one. Crossbowmen took a fearful toll, piling up heaps of bodies before their positions.

Everyone who could be spared from the fighting struggled against the fires. Since water was precious, they had to douse the fires with handfuls of dirt. In order to prevent the fires' spread, sections of wall had to be torn down, exposing the defenders nearby to enemy missiles.

The Spaniards were surprised to learn that the Aztecs had lost their fear of guns. Once they understood that they were the weapons of mortal men, they charged straight at the flaming muzzles. Each volley cut wide furrows through the mass of warriors. But although the Aztecs suffered terribly, they immediately filled the gaps and kept coming. During lulls in the fighting, they kept up the pressure with bloodcurdling cries and shouted descriptions of what they'd do to the Spaniards when they captured them.

The fighting was an eye-opener for Cortes's veterans. They had become overconfident, too used to having the Aztecs submit to their will. At last they understood why they were so feared by other tribes. The Aztecs were the greatest fighting people they'd met in the New World.

The Spaniards counterattacked several times during the following days. They'd gather unnoticed behind the palace gate, then storm out to break the encirclement. They never succeeded for more than a few minutes at a time. They'd drive the Indians up the narrow streets, only to be showered with rocks, even boulders, from the flat rooftops. Every house had been turned into a fort, impossible to capture without battling for each room. Fire was useless, because the adobe houses burned slowly and the canals prevented the blaze from spreading to nearby buildings.

Bernal Diaz and his comrades grew to respect the enemy.

> We noted their tenacity in fighting, but I declare that I do not know how to describe it, for neither cannon nor muskets nor crossbows availed, nor hand-to-hand fighting, nor killing thirty or forty of them every time we charged, for they still fought on in as close ranks and with more energy than in the beginning. Sometimes when we were gaining a little ground or a part of the street, they pretended to retreat, but it was merely to induce us to follow them and cut us off from our fortress and quarters, so as to fall on us in greater safety to themselves, believing that we could not return to our quarters alive, for they did us so much damage when we were retreating.
>
> As to going out to burn their houses, I have already said that between one house and another they have wooden drawbridges, and these they raised so that we could only pass through deep water. Then we could not endure the rocks and stones hurled from the roofs, in such a way that they damaged and wounded many of our men. I do not know why I write thus, so lukewarmly, for some three or four soldiers who were there with us and who had served in Italy, swore to God many times that they had never seen such fierce fights, not even when they had taken part in such between Christians and against the artillery of the King of France, or of the Great Turk, nor had they seen like those Indians with such courage in closing up their ranks.

The steady hail of rocks did more harm than the Aztecs' other weapons put together. Flint points and obsidian blades shattered against steel armor. But rocks smashed helmets and cracked skulls. A rock paralyzed two fingers of Cortes's left hand for life.

After that experience, Cortes had carpenters build several *tortugas*—turtles. He'd borrowed the idea from the ancient Romans, masters at building war machines. A turtle was simply a tall wooden-beamed box with a roof, mounted

Cortes built tall wooden towers on wheels to be used in clearing the rooftops of Aztecs who threw rocks and spears at the Spaniards in the streets below. The towers, although strongly built, were easily toppled and set afire by the Indians. (Redrawn from the Lienzo de Tlaxcala.)

on wheels, with space inside for twenty musketeers and crossbowmen. When pushed through the streets, the soldiers, firing through slits in the walls, would be able to clear the rockthrowers from the roofs.

That's not what happened. Warriors broke through the cavalry screen, toppled the clumsy machines, and set them afire.

The Aztecs were always giving their enemies new things to worry about. Hundreds of warriors and armed priests set up a position on the great pyramid and began to lob arrows into the Spanish quarters on the other side of the Serpent Wall. Cannon were useless against them; the pyramid was too close, making it impossible to fire at an angle sharp enough to sweep the top. The enemy had to be driven off in hand-to-hand fighting.

Cortes led the attack in person. It was rough going even before the Spaniards reached the base of the pyramid. The flagstones of the square were smooth and slick with blood, causing the horses to fall. When the Spaniards started up the pyramid, its defenders rolled heavy logs down on them. The soldiers had to leap from side to side, or tilt the logs out of the way with halberds. Some weren't quick enough and paid with their lives.

The attackers reached the summit, only to find themselves in a shouting, stabbing, free-for-all. Spaniard and Aztec grappled, often tumbling over the edge, locked together as their bodies bounced down the steps to the flagstones below.

Cortes hacked his way into the temple and, seeing Huitzilopochtli standing in place of the Virgin Mary, ordered the place burned. The sight of the leaping flames drove the Aztecs into a frenzy. Gradually, however, steel shattered flint and the Spaniards gained the upper hand. Those Indians who weren't killed outright were hurled over the edge, as were the wounded. None survived.

"Oh! What a fight and what a fierce battle it was that took that place," Bernal Diaz exclaimed. "It was a memorable thing to see all of us streaming with blood and covered with wounds and others slain."

Cortes counterattacks. After being beseiged in Lord Water Monster's palace, Cortes led a raiding party of Spaniards and Tlaxcalans to drive the Aztecs from the top of the Great Pyramid, from which they fired arrows into the Spanish position. The temple of Hummingbird Wizard has already been set on fire, although the Jaguar and Eagle Knights beneath the roof don't seem to have noticed the flames. (Redrawn from the Lienzo de Tlaxcala.)

A Spaniard sets fire to the temples of Huitzilopochtli and Tlaloc atop the great pyramid of Tenochtitlan. (Redrawn from the Lienzo de Tlaxcala.)

Cortes knew that more "victories" like this would destroy his army. Simple arithmetic was against them. The Spaniards were losing fifty to sixty men a day, killed and wounded. Even if the Aztecs lost ten times that number, they'd finally be able to annihilate their enemies. Besides, the Spaniards were no longer united. Navarez's men had come to Tenochtitlan expecting an easy time, wealth dropping into their hands without a struggle. Now that they were fighting for their lives, they cursed Cortes to his face. He didn't dare punish them for fear of triggering a mutiny.

For the last time Cortes turned to Montezuma for help. Messengers were sent to tell him that he must go up on the roof and persuade his people to stop fighting. If he succeeded, the Spaniards would leave the city, never to return.

Montezuma had heard too many of Cortes's promises to believe this one. "What does Malinche want of me?" he moaned. "I want neither to live nor to listen to him."

After a private talk with Padre Olmedo, he agreed to go. He dressed carefully in his most beautiful clothes and ornaments. He wanted to look his best, for something told him that this was the last time he'd see his people.

Montezuma stepped onto the roof, surrounded by a bodyguard of Spaniards. He stood erect, staring down at the crowd, without saying a word. The people, seeing him, fell silent.

For a long moment they stood quietly, staring at each other. Then the Angry Young Lord, he whose voice had made enemies tremble, spoke. He told of his love for the people, and how that love made him go to live with the strangers. He begged them to stop fighting and allow them to leave. Let there be an end to the killing.

Several chiefs stepped from the crowd. They were crying. "Great Lord," said one, "we feel deeply for you in your misfortune. But we have had to raise up one of your kinsmen, Cuitlahac, to be our lord in your place. The war must go on. We have vowed to the gods not to stop until the white men are all dead. We pray to Huitzilopochtli every day to guard you and save you from the white men. Please forgive us."

Others weren't so kind. "Cowardly woman!" someone shouted, looking straight at him. "Weakling . . . rascal . . . coward!" rose from the crowd. A warrior—we'll never know who—notched an arrow to a bowstring. The arrow flew, followed by a shower of arrows and stones.

The soldiers guarding Montezuma had lowered their shields during the speeches, as he seemed safe. Suddenly a stone hit him on the head, another on the arm, a third on the leg.

They carried him to his room unconscious. Surgeons revived him and bandaged his wounds, but he tore them off each time. Although the wounds didn't seem serious, he grew steadily worse. Padre Olmedo tried to convert him to

Christianity to save his soul, but he remained faithful to the Aztec gods.

Montezuma died three days after being wounded, June 29, 1520. The true cause of death wasn't anything a surgeon could see. The fatal wound lay deep inside the man, in his spirit. The Aztec ruler died of shame and grief and a broken heart.

～   ～   ～

The Spaniards were in a tight spot. If they remained in Tenochtitlan, they'd either starve or be killed. The only thing to do was to evacuate the city without delay.

Cortes made his plans carefully. The shortest causeway, the one leading west to Tacuba, was only about two miles long. Eight canals cut the causeway, but scouts reported that the bridges over them had been removed. This was no problem for the cavalry, for men on horseback could jump some of the gaps and swim their horses across the others. Alvarado and Sandoval even led a patrol to Tacuba, returning with bunches of roses for their commander. He scowled and gave them a tongue-lashing for recklessness.

The main problem was getting across with the infantry and baggage. Cortes ordered the carpenters to build a portable bridge to span the widest canal. He intended for the bridge to be picked up after the army crossed a gap and brought forward to the next one, and so on until it reached the mainland.

At sunset, June 30, 1520, Cortes had the treasure brought from its storeroom and heaped up in the main hall of Lord Water Monster's palace. The treasure, mostly in the form of heavy gold bars and chains, shimmered in the torchlight.

The soldiers lined up to watch as the King's fifth was set aside; it would be transported on the backs of eight lame horses. Cortes's share was given into the care of his servants.

He then told the men, "I can do no more with the rest. It is all yours. Take whatever you think you can carry away.

His words were like an invitation to starving men to share a lavish banquet. They rushed at the treasure, grabbing anything they could lay their hands on. Pockets and packs were stuffed with gold; some even put two or three bars under their helmets.

Navarez's men were especially greedy. None had ever seen such a treasure, and they loaded themselves with as much as seventy-five pounds of loot. Bernal Diaz and other veterans looked on, amused at their comrades' greed. Carefully, they each selected a few pieces of the finest jade, which, they knew, the Indians valued more than gold. Plenty of fighting lay ahead, and they didn't want to be burdened with any more weight than necessary. Jade could always be traded for food in villages along the way, and it wouldn't slow them down if they had to run for their lvies.

Toward midnight, the palace gates swung open and the army filed out. There were twelve hundred fifty Spaniards and at least five thousand Tlaxcalan warriors. In addition, Cortes had about fifty hostages—Aztec nobles and two of Montezuma's daughters.

The army marched in four divisions, each with its own assignment. Cortes and Sandoval led the advance guard on horseback; it would clear the way for the others. Behind them came four hundred Tlaxcalans carrying the bridge on their shoulders. The main body followed with the hostages, baggage, treasure, and cannon. A rear guard, the smallest detachment, was commanded by Alvarado. Cavalry rode up and down the column, ready to help wherever needed.

Cortes's luck seemed to be holding once again. The streets were empty; for some unknown reason the Aztecs had failed to post sentries. It was dark. A fine drizzle fell and patches of fog clung to the ground along the lakeshore.

The column moved silently, like some serpent slithering through the night. It wound along the Serpent Wall and onto the causeway. The cannon wheels were wrapped in rags to muffle the sound. Riders placed one hand over their horse's nostrils to prevent snorting. Nobody spoke.

Arriving at the first canal, the Tlaxcalans put the bridge over the gap. It fit perfectly. The army began to cross.

Cortes's luck changed as quickly as you can turn the page of a book. A woman filling a water jug near the causeway saw the Tlaxcalans arrive. "Mexicans!" she shouted, "Come here quickly! Your enemies are leaving."

Her voice cut through the stillness of the night. It reached the priests standing watch at Huitzilopochtli's temple. The great drum boomed across the city. Within

Giving the alert. As Cortes's army steals out of Tenochtitlan, they are seen by a woman taking water from a canal. Her shouts, represented by the artist as comma-shaped balloons coming from her mouth, are heard by the priest atop the temple. (Redrawn from the Lienzo de Tlaxcala.)

seconds drummers atop the clan pyramids were summoning their warriors.

Angry Indians pressed the fugitives on three sides at once. Canoes by the thousand swarmed on either side of the causeway. The canoemen cast their barbed spears, wicked weapons that cut deep and held tight in the wound like a fishhook. A screaming mob attacked along the causeway itself, breaking through the thin rear guard.

Everything now depended upon the portable bridge, and it failed. The weight of so much traffic had wedged it into the gap, setting it as if in cement. The Tlaxcalans pulled at the corners. Nothing happened. They tried to pry it loose with crowbars. The heavy timbers wouldn't budge. The frightened men dropped their tools and ran away.

The retreating army began to disintegrate. Those who'd crossed the bridge early were able to pass over the remaining gaps on their own. The advance guard, with time to choose their footing, didn't lose a man. All were soaked to the skin, but alive. Those who came later weren't so lucky.

Panic gripped the fugitives as Aztec warriors seemed to pop up everywhere at once. Officers lost control of their men, and men lost control of themselves. The army became a mob, pushing and shoving and cursing its way toward the second gap.

Yawning before them was an opening twelve feet wide and as many feet deep. It might as well have been as wide as the Atlantic Ocean for most of those who saw it gleaming in the moonlight. Those nearest the edge were knocked over by those pressing in from behind: porters with heavy loads on their backs, Spanish infantrymen, Tlaxcalan warriors, horses and riders, baggage and boxes, prisoners and cannon. All tumbled into the gap.

Nearly everyone who slipped into the water was pulled under by their loads or crushed by the people and things that fell on top of them. Cortes's generosity cost hundreds their lives. The gold bars the soldiers carried were too heavy to run with, let alone fight and swim. Many drowned rather than part with their wealth. "They died rich," said the old campaigners mockingly.

Others felt hands reaching down for them. But these weren't helping hands. They were the hands of Aztec warriors greedy for another kind of loot. Half-drowned men, Spanish and Tlaxcalans, were hauled into canoes, tied, and sent ashore to be sacrificed to Huitzilopochtli.

The living crossed over a bridge of corpses and wreckage, only to be pushed into the next gap by those behind *them*.

In the meantime Cortes led the advance guard to shore. He stationed some men at the head of the causeway and, together with Sandoval and a few officers, galloped back to help the struggling survivors. On the way they met Alvarado, who had his own hair-raising tale to tell. The rear guard was nearly wiped out to a man. Alvarado, thrown to the ground when a stone killed his horse, rushed to the gap. Already Indian hands were tearing at the Child of the Sun, eager for the honor of taking such an important prisoner. With no place to go but forward, Alvarado summoned all his strength and ran toward the gap. Thrusting his spear into the water, he pole-vaulted across the gap in full armor. From then on this spot has been called "Alvarado's Leap." Few others had his skill and good luck.

Cortes sat grimly on his horse, watching the remnants of his army stumble along the Tacuba road. All were wounded, and many lame. The only bright spot was the appearance of Doña Marina, tired but otherwise none the worse for her experience. Although big with her captain's child, she'd come through the horror without a scratch.

Everything else was bleakness and despair. Eight hundred fifty Spaniards and at least four thousand Tlaxcalans

*La Noche Triste, the night of sadness, begins. As the Spaniards
and their Tlaxcalan allies flee over the causeway, Aztecs attack
them with spears from canoes on either side. (Redrawn from the
Codex Florentino.)*

were dead. None of the Aztec prisoners survived. Of the horses, twenty-four out of ninety-five remained. All the cannon were gone. Nearly all the muskets and cross-bows were lost; the few that were salvaged had ammunition for only a few shots. The Spaniards had lost their thunder. From now on they'd have to rely on their sharp blades alone.

And they were poor. The King's Fifth and Cortes's share of the treasure had disappeared in the confusion. Many millions of dollars in gold bars are waiting to be uncovered somewhere under today's Mexico City.

It was too much for Cortes to bear. At last the nervous strain and exhaustion of the last few days took hold of him. He dismounted and sat under a twisted old cypress tree by the roadside. There, in the rain, he put his head between his hands and wept. The troops hobbled past, glanced in his direction for a moment, and kept going. All wept, either openly or in their hearts.

Yet the commander couldn't enjoy the comfort of tears for too long. The army was still in grave danger and he must do his duty.

Aztec war parties hung on the army's flanks and rear as it marched toward Tacuba. Although they shot arrows and hurled stones, it was mostly their curses that reached the Spaniards. They kept a respectful distance, not pressing their advantage, for their thoughts were back in Tenochtitlan. The bulk of the Indian forces had remained behind in the capital. The Spaniards were too battered to be dangerous, they thought; plenty of time to finish them off later. Now was the time to praise the gods. The Aztecs spent the rest of the night sacrificing captives by torchlight and in giving thanks for Huitzilopochtli's triumph over his enemies.

By stopping to worship their gods, the Indians gave their foes a new lease on life. The Spaniards, battered and worn out, stumbled into Tacuba and camped in the walled square around a pyramid. Guards were posted while their comrades threw themselves on the ground for a few hours' sleep. Before long the only sounds to be heard were snoring and the crackling of campfires.

So ended the Spaniards' night of sadness. *La Noche Triste*, history has called it ever since.

～ ～ ～

The soldiers rested and dressed their wounds as best they could next day. At nightfall, after lighting fires to deceive Aztec scouts, they continued the retreat under cover of darkness.

Their route lay around the northern tip of the lake, then eastward to Tlaxcala. Cortes didn't know what to expect when—*if*—they reached their destination. The Tlaxcalans had been loyal to him in victory. Would they still be loyal in defeat? Or would they hand him over to the Aztecs as a way of buying peace? Only time would tell.

In the meantime the army trudged on through enemy territory. The countryside was alive with war parties, who pelted the fugitives with arrows and stones. Yet these groups seemed small, and they never pressed an attack. The Spaniards noted their behavior and wondered why. It was unlike the Aztecs to be so timid. Whatever the reason, they were thankful for the breathing spell.

There was plenty to worry about besides war parties. The army resembled a mob of starving cripples. As Cortes later wrote King Charles: "No horse could run, no rider lift up his arms, no foot soldier placed one foot in front of another." The badly wounded had to be left behind to die or kill themselves rather than be captured for sacrifice. The walking wounded hobbled along on crutches or held onto the horses' tails to be dragged along in the choking dust.

The lucky ones were tied in pairs to horses too lame to fight. Everyone else, cavalrymen included, walked. Cortes wanted to save the strength of the healthy mounts for fighting.

Food was always scarce, for all the supplies had been lost on the causeway. The men, dizzy with hunger, ate whatever came their way. They gulped down wild cherries, pits and all. Fat white beetle grubs helped fill empty stomachs. A horse killed in a skirmish was promptly eaten. Nothing was left of it except cracked bones, teeth, and hair. Yet even the starving were expected to behave like Spanish soldiers. A man who tried to eat part of a dead Indian was strung up instantly.

The army marched on like this for six days. On the morning of the seventh day, July 7, 1520, it reached the heights above the Valley of Otumba. The downhill trek was easy, as gravity took over, helping tired muscles. The men became cheerful for the first time since *La Noche Triste*. Up ahead the scouts, turning the corner of a hill, had a clear view of the valley. They froze in their tracks, unable to speak for the moment when they looked into the valley below. At last they understood why the war parties they'd met were so small.

The Aztecs, knowing that Cortes would make for Tlaxcala, had concentrated their forces across his path. Over a hundred thousand Indians covered the valley floor. From one end to the other, the Valley of Otumba was an unbroken sea of headdresses and feather banners.

The *Conquistadores* found themselves between the jaws of an immense trap. Behind, on the other side of the mountains, lay the city in the lake—the city of death. Ahead waited the armed might of the Aztec empire. Incredible as it sounds, Cortes was undaunted by the enormous odds. The man's courage, his fighting spirit, his faith that God favored his venture, seemed without limit. God, he felt, would watch over His stout *Conquistadores*. There was only one thing to do—attack!

Cortes gave the army its battle instructions. It was to advance as a hollow wedge, wounded in the center, infantry in front, cavalry on either flank. Horsemen were not to stop to spear the enemy, but aim at faces and eyes. Foot soldiers should stab, not slash, aiming for their opponents' chests and guts. Musketeers and crossbowmen were to use up their remaining ammunition and join their comrades with swords.

The *Conquistadores* prayed and moved forward. As they stepped onto the battlefield, Cortes cried, "Now, gentlemen of Spain, let us cut our way through them, and leave none of them without a wound!"

From the Aztec ranks came the swish of arrows and stones flying through the air. Calmly the Spaniards raised their shields to brush aside the first volley.

"Santiago! Santiago and at them!" they shouted.

Not to be outdone, their Tlaxcalan friends replied with "Tlaxcala! Santiago! Tlaxcala!"

At first the battle seemed to energize the exhausted men. Danger called forth reserves of strength and courage, teaching them things they'd never known about themselves.

The Aztecs pressed them so closely that it wasn't a matter of one army against another, but of man against man. The *Conquistadores* inched forward, leaving behind a trail of dead and dying Aztecs. Their actions became automatic, as if their muscles knew what to do without instructions from the brain. Block with the shield. Lunge with the blade. Pull out the bloody metal then block and lunge again.

Hours passed, and the sun rose high in the sky. The Spaniards broiled in their armor. Hungry men forgot the gnawing in their stomachs. They fought and sweated.

Yet each step forward only drove them deeper into the Aztec mass. It was only a matter of time until their energy gave out and they were overwhelmed. They needed a miracle.

Cortes, or a power greater than he, saved the day. In the distance, surrounded by a bodyguard, he saw an Indian in a gorgeous costume of gold, jade, and feathers. It was none other than the Snake Woman, next to the Chief Speaker the Aztecs' supreme commander.

Instantly a plan flashed into Cortes's mind. Shouting above the din of battle, he rallied a handful of officers—Sandoval, Cristobal de Olid, Alonzo de Avila, Juan de Salamanca—and charged. They plowed through Snake Woman's bodyguard.

It was a mad dash, too fast for the mind to take in everything that happened. Twice Cortes fell from his horse, only to find himself back in the saddle without knowing who'd helped him up. Still he was first through the bodyguard and slammed his mount full force into the Aztec commander, sending him sprawling. As Snake Woman tumbled head over heels, Juan de Salamanca speared him to the ground and seized his banner. Seeing their commander sprawled dead, the Indians' courage oozed away. The gods had spoken. Leaderless, panic spread through their ranks and they fled.

The *Conquistadores* and their Tlaxcalan friends had done the "impossible." Men flopped to the ground, panting and numb with fatigue. In the distance glimmered the mountains surrounding Tlaxcala. Next day they crossed the border.

Chief Xicotenga came to welcome them. "Oh! Malinche, Malinche!" he said, weeping. "How we grieve for your misfortunes and for your brothers and for those of our own people that have been killed with yours. . . . Do not think, Malinche, that you have done little to escape with your lives from that city and its bridges. I tell you, that if we formerly looked upon you as very brave, we now think you much more so. . . . Rest, Malinche, rest, for you are at home."

5 Fall of an Empire

◎◎◎

A week after arriving in Tlaxcala, Cortes sat down to write his king. It was the hardest letter he'd ever had to write, for it meant reliving past tragedies. He told of battles, retreats, and sufferings. But he also looked forward to better times. One day, he promised, this land, which he'd named New Spain of the Ocean Sea, would be Spain's greatest overseas possession. In closing, he said: "I intend to return to that country and its great city . . . and thus all our past losses shall be made good."

This sounds like the babblings of a madman. His army was a wreck, without cannon or gunpowder. Its remaining horses were tired bags of bones, better suited to the cooking pot than the battlefield. Returning to Tenochtitlan would be like a flea attacking an elephant.

Yet that sentence was no empty boast. Rather, it tells us of the unbreakable courage that lay at the core of the man. Hernan Cortes may have been many things—fanatic, liar, killer. But he was no quitter. He never gave in to defeat or self-doubt. He'd fight, and keep fighting until he won. That was the way of Extremadura.

Rebuilding wasn't easy. Cortes found that his Spaniards were really two armies as different as day is from night. The first was those veterans who'd come with him from Cuba. As the Romans used to say, they were few, but they were eagles. They were the survivors, the best, the bravest of the brave. They had taken the enemy's hardest blows and come through. No longer merely soldiers, they were brothers. Each had proven himself to the others. Thus they trusted one another, depended upon one another, would risk their lives for one another. But most of all they trusted the somber man with the blue-black beard. He'd lead and they'd follow—anywhere.

Navarez's ex-soldiers, the second army, were fair-weather fighters. They'd gone to Mexico because of Cortes's promises of gold and glory. Now they were bruised, battered, and bitter. A petition was handed to the commander demanding that the army withdraw to Villa Rica and try somehow to return to Cuba.

Cuba to Cortes meant Governor Velasquez and the hangman's rope. King Charles still hadn't approved of his actions, although he'd accepted his gold. In the eyes of the law he was still a traitor. But most of all "Cuba" would mean acknowledging defeat.

Cortes assembled the complainers for a pep talk. This time he appealed not to their greed, but to their pride as men. He reminded them that anything worthwhile has to be earned with work, even hardship. All great peoples had known defeat, but had risen above the troubles of the moment. To return to Cuba now would be running away. Of course that sounded appealing now, when they still felt the sting of defeat. But when the pain passed, they'd still have the memory of what they'd done. They'd never outlive the shame of deserting their commander and comrades when they needed them most. Wherever they went, people would recognize them and throw their dishonor into their teeth.

Running away was cowardly. It was un-Spanish. "Never yet, in this New World, have Spanish men turned back for fear, nor for hunger, nor for wounds. God forbid! It is not numbers in battle that count but courage. Courage! It is not the many, but the valiant that win."

Many walked away muttering, but all decided to stay a little longer to see how things went.

Cortes's determination began to have its reward. Tlaxcala became the magnet for every Indian who had something to lose if the Aztecs won. Towns that had helped the Spaniards during the march to Mexico sent warriors to the embattled nation; the Tlaxcalans themselves called up every available man. It was now or never for these Indians. Either they joined forces under Cortes or faced the Aztecs separately. The lords of Tenochtitlan were unforgiving, vengeful, and remembered all who'd turned against them. Cortes soon found himself training over fifty thousand Indians in Spanish fighting methods.

Better yet, Spanish reinforcements began to trickle into camp by way of Villa Rica. Sometimes Cortes benefited from others' mistakes, as when two ships blundered into port with supplies for Navarez; Governor Velasquez still hadn't heard of his lieutenant's defeat. Others came freely, lured by rumors of Mexican treasure. A large merchant-man arrived from Spain with a cargo of muskets, gun-powder, and crossbows. It had been sent by a businessman who saw the chance to make fabulous profits. Cortes, who'd stored some of Montezuma's early gifts in Villa Rica, bought everything without quibbling over price. He also turned on the charm, persuading the crew to jump ship and join him.

Each month brought its quota of adventurers and supplies. Anyone who came with a horse was given a princely welcome and a pocketful of gold. Cortes gladly paid any price for a cannon.

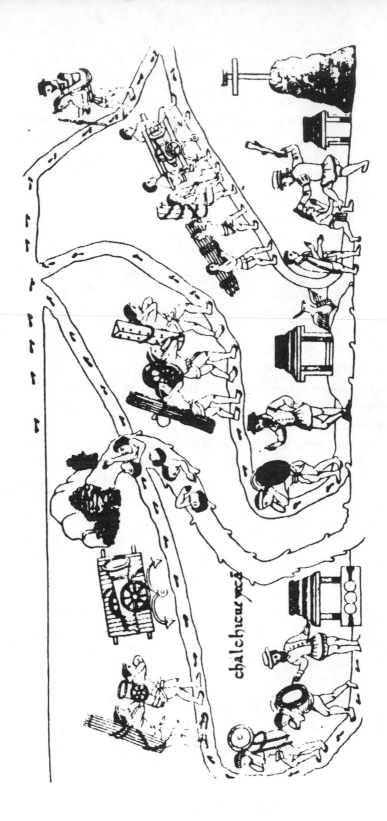

chalchicueyeca

To toughen the newcomers, they were teamed up with veterans and sent on raiding expeditions. Young Sandoval led them against the Tepeacans, a neighboring people allied to the Aztecs. Other captains led hit-and-run attacks into Quechola (Cay-cho-la). Wherever they went, the raiders brought terror and destruction. Indian warriors were slaughtered and their villages burned. Women and children were enslaved. The Spaniards branded them on the cheeks or lips with the letter G for *guerra*—war. Some were made to work for their captors, the rest sold at auction. Cortes, as captain-general, always took a share of the profits.

Everyone learned valuable lessons from these raids. The army developed self-confidence and teamwork. The Indian allies saw that they were backing a winner after all. And their victims realized that loyalty to the Aztecs didn't pay, because their masters couldn't protect them. Word spread into the Valley of Mexico that the Spaniards would stop at nothing to have their way.

Raids were part of a long-range plan for destroying Aztec power. Cortes analyzed his own defeat carefully, determined to learn from past mistakes. *La Noche Triste* haunted his dreams. He saw again the canoes filled with warriors who cut down his men as they jammed the narrow causeway. The lake, obviously, held the key to the entire campaign. Controlling its waters would protect his forces while trapping the Aztecs on their island. Cortes meant to turn Tenochtitlan's first line of defense to his own advantage.

◀ *This picture-map by an Indian artist tells about Cortes's preparation to return to the Valley of Mexico in 1521. On the right, bottom, a Spaniard is disciplining unruly Indians at Villa Rica de la Vera Cruz. Other Indians are carrying supplies to be used in the invasion. The Indian in the upper right is carrying a Spaniard over the mountains from the coast. (Picture redrawn from the Lienzo de Tlaxcala.)*

To do this, he decided to build thirteen brigantines, small, swift vessels powered by oars and sails, easily maneuvered in shallow waters. Each brigantine would have a crew of Indian rowers and a Spanish sailing master. A light cannon in the bow, plus musketeers and crossbowmen, would supply the firepower.

The building project was assigned to Martin Lopez, an experienced ship's carpenter. Lopez took hundreds of Indian laborers into the hills around Tlaxcala to cut tall oak and pine trees. After stripping the bark, the tree trunks were split lengthwise into planks, then planed smooth and made square. Soon masts were poking skyward from forest clearings. When the ships were ready, Lopez had them dismantled and each piece numbered for reassembly later. The vessels that Cortes had scuttled the year before now came to life in a different form. Their ironware, cordage, and canvas were brought over the mountains from Villa Rica on the backs of Indian porters for use in the brigantines.

On December 26, 1520, the day after Christmas and six months after *La Noche Triste*, Cortes was ready to return to the Valley of Mexico. His army had been entirely rebuilt. He had over nine hundred Spaniards, among them one hundred eighteen musketeers and crossbowmen. The cavalry, the sixteenth-century version of a tank corps, numbered ninety horses and riders. The artillery mustered fifteen small bronze guns and three heavy iron cannon—wall smashers. The porters didn't have to lug iron cannon balls, since artillery in those days fired mostly stones shaped on the spot to fit individual gun barrels.

In addition to the Spaniards, Cortes commanded no fewer than fifty thousand Tlaxcalans, plus uncounted thousands of warriors from other tribes. Supporting the fighters were seventy thousand Indian laborers to carry supplies, build roads, and do the countless other chores of an army in the field. Without these Indian auxiliaries,

Cortes couldn't even have thought of attacking the Aztecs in their stronghold.

The commander held a review of his forces and issued orders to govern it during the campaign. There were plenty of nos: no gambling, quarreling, disobedience, attacking without orders. Bad language was un-Christian and wouldn't be tolerated. Any soldier who said "damn it," for instance, would be fined in gold. All booty had to be turned over to Cortes on pain of death.

Once again he announced that they were making war not for profit, but for God and against the devil. As Christians, they had a responsibility to God for the Aztecs' souls, said Cortes. "If we convert them from idolatry to a knowledge of our holy faith, God will be pleased with the saving of so many souls from damnation, and we shall not only win glory everlasting but we shall also have God's help in this world." That is, the Lord would make them rich.

∾   ∾   ∾

As before, the *Conquistadores* marched westward over the mountains into the Valley of Mexico. Their first objective was not Tenochtitlan, but Texcoco on the eastern shore of the lake. The second city of the valley, Texcoco was one of ancient America's centers of art and learning. Although it was one of the original members of the Aztec alliance, in recent years it had grown to resent its partner in the lake, for Montezuma, at the height of his power, replaced the lord of Texcoco with one of his own relatives.

The Texcocans never forgave this insult and were now about to repay the favor. At the invaders' approach, they surrendered their city without a struggle. Cortes immediately made it his base of operations against Tenochtitlan. Strong detachments fanned out to the lakeside communities and to those deep in the countryside beyond. Any town that resisted was taken by storm, looted, and its people massacred or enslaved. Before long, scores of towns opened their gates rather than face the conqueror's anger.

The hardest fighting was in towns with Aztec garrisons. Warriors would barricade themselves in a temple enclosure and fight to the last men. Though starving, they shouted that they didn't need food, because they'd soon be feasting upon the Spaniards and their friends.

Cortes was now up against his most determined enemy. The Aztec leadership had changed since *La Noche Triste*. The weeks following it were also sad ones for the victorious Indians, for as the Spaniards retreated, they left behind millions of invisible allies, who killed silently and without mercy.

One of Navarez's men was a Negro infected with smallpox he'd caught in Cuba. The disease affected people in different ways. Europeans, who'd been exposed to smallpox germs for centuries, had developed a natural resistance to the disease. Many still died, of course, but most survived after running a high fever. The faces of nearly all Europeans of Cortes's time were pitted with small holes, scars caused by dried fever sores.

Nothing like smallpox existed in the New World before 1492. The Indians, lacking any immunity, were hit full force. Wherever Europeans went, epidemics struck without warning or explanation. "They died in heaps, like bedbugs," wrote a Spanish doctor.

For sixty days after *La Noche Triste*, smallpox raged through Tenochtitlan. At the very moment Cortes's army was licking its wounds in Tlaxcala, their enemies were battling the epidemic. They didn't know what to do. People, burning with fever, plunged into the lake and drowned. Others, covered with tiny sores, were driven mad by the itching. Hundreds went blind.

Among those who died was the new Chief Speaker, Cuitlahuac. In his place the tribal council elected his nephew, Cuauhtemoc (Kwow-ta'y-moc). At twenty-one, Falling Eagle (for that's what the name means) was in the prime of life. Handsome, a born leader and fighter, he was adored by the people.

Falling Eagle was determined to save his Aztec heritage or pull the world down around him in ruins. There'd be no talking or dealings with the hated foreigners. His struggle became a symbol of courage to future generations of Mexicans. His statue stands today atop a tall column in the center of Mexico City, and pictures of him hang in people's homes beside those of Benito Juarez and other later heroes of Mexican independence.

Cortes sent messengers to Cuauhtemoc with offers of peace. His messages were filled with honeyed words. He

Smallpox, Cortes's invisible ally, killed thousands of people in Tenochtitlan after La Noche Triste. *Here we see people covered from head to toe with the tiny sores. (Redrawn from the Codex Florentino.)*

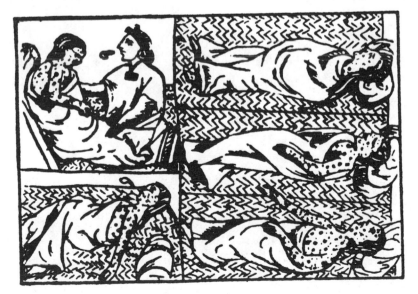

The heads of Spaniards and their horses were displayed by the Aztec leaders to show the people that their enemies were mortal, not divine creatures from another world. (Redrawn from the Codex Florentino.)

loved the Aztecs and didn't want to bring them pain, he said. If they surrendered immediately, he'd treat them with respect and generosity. If they refused his "kindnss," it would mean a war of annihilation.

Falling Eagle closed his ears both to the enemy's promises and threats. The first he didn't believe for a moment, the second he knew were only too sincere. His reply came in deeds, not words. Food was stockpiled in the public warehouses. Allies who joined the war were released from future tribute payments. The heads of Spaniards and horses taken during *La Noche Triste* were sent to outlying villages to quiet fears that the invaders were gods.

∾   ∾   ∾

Cortes's preparations went ahead like clockwork. One day a column of Tlaxcalan laborers six miles long arrived with the dismantled brigantines. In order to protect them from Aztec war parties, they were reassembled in a shipyard built in the hills two miles from the lakeshore. As Martin Lopez's craftsmen went about their work, laborers began to deepen a nearby stream, turning it into a canal.

Sunday, April 28, 1521, was a memorable day. The last earthen barriers were shoveled away, connecting the canal with the lake. As Padre Olmedo led the soldiers in prayer, laborers knocked the supports out from under the brigantines. One by one the vessels slid downhill into the lake. Striking the water in a cloud of spray, they bobbed about wildly for a moment, then steadied themselves. Martin Lopez had reason to be proud of himself.

Most of May was spent in arming the vessels and rigging their sailing gear. Spanish and Tlaxcalan crews gained their "sea legs" in cruises along the Texcocan shore. Had an Aztec war fleet appeared, they would have dashed out of the way or huddled under the shore batteries for protection. Cortes was unwilling to risk a fight until the crews were familiar with their craft.

On May 26, 1521, he struck. Pedro de Alvarado and Cristobal de Olid burst into Tacuba with their horsemen. After a brief skirmish with the defenders, they used axes and crowbars to wreck the aqueduct that supplied the capital with water from Chapultepec. From now on Tenochtitlan's teeming population would have to rely on a couple of tiny springs or drink salt water. It was the beginning of the end of the proud city in the lake.

Six days later, June 1, Cortes sailed with the fleet. As it glided past a small, rocky island, signal fires flared from a hilltop, warning the capital of its approach. Cortes shouted for the sailing masters to drop anchor and led his men in storming the hilltop. They had just wiped out the

*Spanish brigantines, small sailing vessels able to maneuver easily
in shallow water, played a key role in isolating and destroying
Tenochtitlan. (Redrawn from the Codex Florentino.)*

Aztec defenders when they noticed a fleet of over a thousand war canoes bearing down on them from Tenochtitlan. The lookouts' message had been received.

The Spaniards hastily reboarded their ships and took up battle stations. But instead of moving forward, as everyone expected, Cortes ordered the sailing masters to hold the vessels motionless so as to make the enemy think they were frightened.

The Aztec fleet drew up a short distance away, unsure of how to deal with these strange vessels. The Spaniards stared at them nervously, remembering how those same canoes had terrorized them during *La Noche Triste*. Nobody wanted to repeat that experience.

Just then a stiff land breeze sprang up, filling the ships' sails. The heavy vessels plowed into the massed canoes, shattering them to splinters. The sound of crunching wood mingled with the roar of gunfire and the cries of men. Within seconds the water was churning with Indians struggling to save their lives.

Few succeeded. The Spaniards, out to avenge *La Noche Triste*, took no prisoners. As the brigantines sailed by, soldiers leaned over to stab warriors floundering in the water. "It was the most wonderful sight in the world to behold!" wrote Bernal Diaz. The pursuit continued until the remaining canoes disappeared into the city's winding canals.

Cortes went on to blockade Tenochtitlan by water and land. Day and night his ships swept the lake of enemy canoes. Aztec oarsmen were no match for their sails *and* oars. The brigantines easily ran down and destroyed canoes bringing food to the city from the mainland.

On land, Cortes divided his army into three units, one for each of the causeways. Olid took charge of the southern approaches. Alvarado blocked the Tabuca causeway in the west. Sandoval commanded at Tepeyac, the northern causeway. Cortes directed operations from headquarters aboard the fleet. It was as if he'd flung a noose around the city and was tightening it slowly.

At first the Spaniards looked forward to battle. A friendly rivalry developed among the commanders to see who'd penetrate deepest into the city. Yet as the month of June passed, it became clear that the Aztecs still had plenty of fight left in them.

The Spaniards became bogged down in endless skirmishes that led nowhere. Each day's fighting seemed a carbon copy of the one before, only more difficult. The Spaniards and their allies would advance along a causeway, only to halt before a gap where a bridge had stood. That meant several hours of throwing in wood, corn stalks, and bundles of reeds to make a passage across.

Once inside the city, the troops, already tired from their labors, had to fight every inch of the way. Sometimes, if they were lucky, they did serious damage, burning food stockpiles and destroying water supplies. The palaces of Lord Water Monster and Montezuma went up in flames, taking the royal aviaries and zoo along with them.

But the invaders were never able to hold on to captured ground. The city itself helped the Aztecs by concealing their movements. The Spanish horses, so dangerous in the open, became easy targets in the narrow streets. Everywhere the line of march passed beneath rooftops, from which the defenders hurled stones. The buildings were screens, allowing warriors to sneak up behind an advancing column, forcing it to retreat. When they returned to the attack next morning, they found that the Indians had reopened the gaps in the canals during the night.

The Aztecs nearly captured the hated Alvarado during one of these skirmishes. On June 23, 1521, the Child of the Sun set out across the Tacuba causeway with several hundred soldiers and warriors. After filling in the gaps,

Time and again Cortes's brigantines came in close to shore to use their cannon to break up concentrations of Indians. Indian arrows were no match for artillery. (Redrawn from the Codex Florentino.)

they charged down one of the main avenues. It was a grand, stirring charge. All the excited men could see was Aztecs fleeing ahead of them. They chased them as fast as they could, certain that victory was within reach.

What Alvarado's men couldn't see were the thousands of hidden warriors. Hundreds of others, meanwhile, were landing from canoes in the rear to reopen the canal gap and plant pointed stakes underwater.

Suddenly the fleeing Aztecs stopped and turned. Their comrades burst from cover, unleashing a storm of arrows and stones. Alvarado's men fled in terror, only to be driven into the water and onto the stakes. Many died there, or were hauled out for sacrifice.

Bernal Diaz, who'd fought in every battle thus far, was lucky to escape with only a deep shoulder wound. He was wading into the water when Indians suddenly bowled him over from behind. They were grappling with him, trying to slip his wrists into a noose, when he cried out to God for mercy. That prayer seemed to renew his energy. Somehow he freed his sword arm and cut his way to safety.

Cortes decided to revenge this setback with an all-out attack. His plan called for a co-ordinated assault in which Sandoval, Alvarado, and Olid would advance at the same time. Their columns were to punch across the city, linking up in the Tlatelolco marketplace. There was plenty of room there for the whole army; the cavalry could maneuver easily in the large open space. If all went well, the Aztecs would be boxed into the northeastern corner of the island, between his forces and the lake. They'd have to surrender.

The attack began at dawn, June 30, 1521. It was the first anniversary of *La Noche Triste* and Spanish spirits were high. They were attacking in strength and nothing could stop them, they thought. Although they couldn't know it when the trumpets sounded, this day would be as sad as that night had been.

At first everything went according to plan. Alvarado and Sandoval moved steadily forward against light resistance. The problem was on the southern front, where the attackers advanced in three columns along parallel streets that ended at a broad canal near the Tlatelolco marketplace.

The column on the left was led by a man named

Spanish positions and commanders during the siege of Tenochtitlan

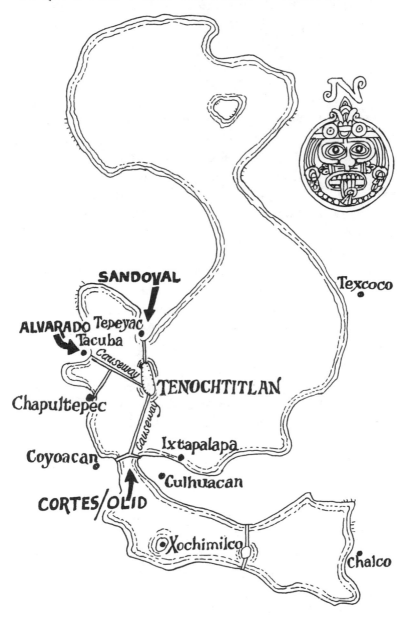

Alderete. Eager for the honor of being first into Tlatelolco, Alderete pushed his column faster than the others. Once across the canal, he sent a message asking the commander's permission to go on to the marketplace. Cortes, thinking it odd that he'd advanced faster than the others, rode to the crossing point to find the reason.

He had warned his captains that, whatever happened, they must protect their line of retreat. They mustn't advance a step without making sure that the causeway gaps were solidly filled. Although Alderete hadn't disobeyed orders, he hadn't obeyed them fully either. The canal was lightly filled with scrap wood and corn stalks. This mess had carried the weight of men crossing in good order, with time to choose their footing, but it could never bear men and horses fleeing in panic.

A commotion across the canal showed Cortes that what he feared most was happening. The Aztecs had watched the enemy's advance, waiting to throw their strength against one of the columns. They chose Alderete's.

His men came rushing toward the canal, the Aztecs close on their heels. The makeshift bridge collapsed under the weight of the first arrivals, opening a gap ten paces wide with water flowing through it ten feet deep.

It was a horrifying, howling, pile-in, just like *La Noche Triste*. Men sank by the score as they hit the water, dragged under by the weight of their armor. Cortes and the men with him did what they could to help the unfortunates. But they were soon fighting for their own lives.

More Aztec warriors were landed behind them from canoes and these immediately recognized Cortes. Here was an offering to gladden Huitzilopochtli!

A dozen warriors pounced on the Spaniard. For a moment Cortes lost control of himself. He slashed at the Indians with his sword while holding out his hand to a drowning soldier. "Hold on!" he roared, "Hold on!"

Seeing him surrounded, a captain named Antonio Quiñones leaped to his side. Cortes saw him and knew that he wanted to help, but he seemed unable to help himself. He continued to fight and reach out to the drowning man.

Quiñones cut down an Indian and, grabbing his commander's arm, shouted full in his face: "Let us get away from here and save yourself, for you know that without you none of us will escape." Those words snapped him out of his daze and he allowed his companions to lead him to safety. Quiñones was right, he knew. For the army would disintegrate without his leadership and example.

The fight at the Tlatelolco canal was a disaster. The southern division lost at least forty Spaniards killed and over a thousand Indian allies; sixty-five Spaniards were captured and hauled away for sacrifice.

The battle, however, was only beginning for Alvarado and Sandoval. Alderete's defeat freed thousands of Aztec warriors, who moved speedily across town to fight them. While shouting insults at Alvarado's men, they flung in front of them five heads streaming with blood. The heads, they cried, belonged to Malinche and Sandoval. Likewise, Sandoval's column was greeted with heads said to be those of Malinche and Alvarado. The hardpressed Spaniards, unsure of whose heads they were, retreated in good order.

Once again, as during *La Noche Triste*, the Aztecs let the enemy escape. A European general, whose victorious soldiers outnumbered a beaten enemy, would have kept fighting until they were completely destroyed or night came to end the battle, but this was not the Aztec way. Prayers must be said, sacrifices made, and victory dances held.

The fleeing Spaniards were amazed when the pursuit slackened. Instead, the snakeskin drum of Huitzilopochtli boomed dismally over the lake, drowning out the sounds of battle. Looking up, the Spaniards saw their friends being herded up the side of the great pyramid. Let Bernal Diaz describe what happened next:

> (We) saw that our comrades whom they had captured when they defeated Cortes were being carried by force up the steps, and they were taking them to be sacrificed. When they got them up to a small square in front of the temple, where their accursed idols are kept, we saw them place plumes on the heads of many of them and with things like fans in their hands they forced them to dance before Huichilobos, and after they danced they immediately placed them on their backs on some rather narrow stones which had been prepared as places of sacrifice, and with stone knives they sawed open their chests and drew out their palpitating hearts and offered them to the idols that were there.

The Spaniards stood on the causeway, stunned. Tears sprang to their eyes. Tough as they were, these *Conquistadores* weren't ashamed of crying in public when deeply moved. No one thought less of them for their tears, because men in the sixteenth century showed their feelings more openly than nowadays.

This defeat left them shaken as never before. Diaz, that honest man, admitted to being afraid that someday the same would happen to him. He'd already had some close calls and wondered how long it would please God to spare him. From then on feelings of despair and terror gripped him before going into battle. And he wasn't alone.

～　　～　　～

Cortes had hoped to take Tenochtitlan intact; he thought it "the loveliest city in the world," a worthy capital for New Spain. But the battles of June made him change his mind. He finally realized that there was no shortcut to victory. The city could not be captured in a single blow. It would have to be destroyed totally before its people surrendered.

This decision cheered his Indian allies. They despised the Aztecs, having old scores to settle with them. Apart from killing them, nothing pleased them more than tearing apart their capital, the home of their gods and symbol of their pride.

What the invaders lacked in modern wrecking machinery they made up for with willing hands. At sun-up seventy thousand laborers swarmed over the causeways for the day's work. Like the jaws of an enormous steam shovel, they began to chew away at the fringes of the city, turning it into a wasteland. To the ear-splitting sounds of battle were added the equally chilling noises of destruction. Under the protection of Spanish soldiers, they attacked with axe, shovel, and crowbar. Gangs of workmen attached ropes to building support beams and pulled. The thud of crashing buildings—palaces, temples, warehouses, homes—filled the air until sunset. A cloud of dust and ash hung over the city, smudging the blue sky.

The materials that had once built the city were now used to destroy it. Causeway gaps were permanently filled with rubble, packed tight and stomped into place. Rooftops from which the defenders threw stones disappeared, along with the houses that supported them. The leveled areas that resulted from all this destruction gave the cavalry room to maneuver and charge.

These areas became "killing grounds," places that attracted the enemy and where he could be easily slaughtered. The Aztecs, maddened by the destruction of their city, attacked the wrecking crews. Immediately the call went out for Spanish reinforcements, who rode them down or mowed them down in crossfire.

Cortes began to see signs that his siege methods were working. Cut off from the mainland, the Aztecs were starving. Anything able to give nourishment was eaten: rats, lizards, insects, grass, tanned hides. People gnawed the bark of trees, or filled their stomachs with lumps of clay. Thirst also took its toll, as the few springs on the island were ruined and the people forced to drink salty lake water. Bodies were everywhere. At the start of the siege, when people still had their strength, the dead were disposed of with full religious rites. But as the fighting continued, and the number of dead increased, they were simply hidden inside ruined houses. Finally they were left where they fell. Tenochtitlan became a vast graveyard, and smelled like a mountain of garbage cooking in the sun.

Their bodies were weakening, but the people's fighting spirit remained strong as ever. Again and again Cortes sent messengers to Cuauhtemoc, begging him to give up the hopeless struggle. His answer was always the same. No surrender. No peace with the invader. Not as long as one Aztec remained alive. "It is better," he said, "that we should all die in this city than to fall into the Spaniards' hands to become slaves and to be tortured for gold." Cuauhtemoc had seen enough of the strangers' ways to know what would happen if they ever got his people completely in their power.

The more Cortes spoke of surrender, the harder the Aztecs fought. Archers shot the Spaniards' own arrows back from captured crossbows. Warriors learned how to deal with cannon. When they saw that a gun was about to fire, everyone in its path dropped to the ground and lay flat, allowing the ball to pass harmlessly overhead. They set ambushes for the brigantines. Strong timbers were sharpened to a point and set just below water level near shore or across the mouth of a canal. While some war canoes lay covered with brushwood along the banks, warriors in others tempted the Spaniards to chase them. When the brigantines snagged on the stakes, Aztecs in the hidden canoes attacked. Although they never destroyed the larger craft, they always managed to kill or wound some of their crewmen. For some unknown reason, the Aztecs never used fire, even though the brigantines' sails and tarred planks would have gone up like tinder.

Despite Aztec bravery, by August, 1521, Tenochtitlan resembled a forested mountain whose base had been swept by fire. Except for smoke-blackened pyramids and the ruins of the Serpent Wall, seven-eighths of the city was a field of flattened rubble. It looked as wasted as any city blasted in the thousand-bomber raids of World War II.

Cortes and his captains finally linked up in Tlatelolco, crowding the survivors into the city's last buildings around the marketplace. War is never glorious, only ugly, but siege warfare is ugliest of all. The people had no food fit for humans, nor water. There was hardly any space in which to stand; in some places one could walk hundreds of yards on bodies without setting foot on the ground. An Aztec poet remembered the scene:

> The ways are strewn with broken lances
> Hair is scattered on all sides,
> The houses are without roofs
> Their walls are reddened.
> Worms swarm in streets and squares
> And the walls are spattered with brains,
> The waters are red, as if dyed.
> And when we drink,
> It is as if we drink liquid saltpeter.

And still they fought, although everyone knew the fight was hopeless. On August 12, 1521, Cortes ordered a general assault. His problem now wasn't the taking of lives, but sparing as many as possible. The Aztecs were so weak that they could be killed almost at will. Cortes wanted to capture ground and force a surrender, for the more people who survived, the more there'd be to build New Spain. His Indian allies, however, wanted only to kill, to avenge centuries of humiliation. On that day forty thousand Aztecs died. The *Conquistadores*, sickened at the slaughter, tried to stop their allies, usually without success. Some sheathed their swords and walked to the rear, mumbling and shaking their heads.

Next morning, August 13, Cortes asked to meet Aztec ambassadors to talk about peace. He pleaded with them to persuade Cuauhtemoc to end his people's suffering. A few hours later they returned with the Chief Speaker's final refusal. "Go back then," said Cortes, "and tell Cuauhtemoc and his people to make ready, for I am now coming to destroy them."

The fighting continued until late in the afternoon. Those that could, tried to escape the doomed city by canoe. Among them was the Chief Speaker in a richly decorated canoe paddled by picked oarsmen. It was gliding across the water when a brigantine commander saw it in the distance. He raced after it, sails billowing, cannon primed. Only the show of force was necessary. Cuauhtemoc surrendered without a fight, pleading with the Spaniards not to harm his family or possessions, but take them to Malinche.

Cortes greeted his prisoner with respect; he'd won a war and now he needed the cooperation of the defeated. Cuauhtemoc bowed to the conqueror and said that he'd done everything in his power to defend his homeland. Motioning to the dagger in the Spaniard's belt, he begged him to stab him with it at once.

Cortes had Doña Marina tell him that the killing was over. Although many had died needlessly, he bore no grudges. The Aztecs were a courageous people, and Spaniards knew how to honor courage even in enemies.

〜　　〜　　〜

The capture of Cuauhtemoc ended the fighting. The end came so suddenly that the absence of noise seemed strange.

The siege had lasted seventy-five days. During this time the air had been filled with a mingling of roaring cannon, shouts, musket shots, screams, whistles, drumming, trumpeting, and the sound of crashing buildings. Then it stopped.

Captured while trying to flee his doomed city, Cuauhtemoc, the last Chief Speaker of the Aztecs, is brought before Cortes. Standing behind the conqueror is the ever-present Doña Marina, his translator. The caption of the picture translates as, "With this event, the Mexicans were finished." (Redrawn from the Lienzo de Tlaxcala.)

The quiet was soon shattered by nature. Night fell, a bleak, starless night. A storm burst over the Valley of Mexico, sending sheets of rain. The big drops pelted the earth like volleys of bullets. The wind howled, perhaps reminding listeners of a wounded animal crying in the darkness. Thunder echoed off the rocky hillsides. Lightning flashes lit up the abandoned pyramids. That night, it is said, the Aztec gods went shrieking into the storm, never to return.

6 The Lords of New Spain

◉◎◉

It was the Spaniards' turn to celebrate. The day after
Falling Eagle's surrender, Cortes gave his officers a victory
banquet. A ship with a cargo of pigs and wine had
anchored at Villa Rica so there was plenty to go around.
The merrymakers ate their fill. And they drank more than
was good for them. Some danced on the tables, clapping
their hands and stomping out wild rhythms. Others rolled
on the ground or passed out, snoring. Men, red-faced and
slobbering, bellowed about how they'd have land and
slaves and *mucho, mucho dinero.*

These drunkards' dreams vanished with the morning
star. They awoke to find that they weren't going to have
"much, much money." A quick search showed that there
was little gold to be found in the ruined city or on its
people. There *should* have been a vast treasure. Although
a fortune had been lost during *La Noche Triste*, the largest
part of Montezuma's treasure had been left behind in the
palace of Lord Water Monster, and it was nowhere to be
found.

175

Cortes had the clan chiefs of Tenochtitlan brought to him for questioning. Fixing them with his grave, gray eyes, he demanded that they produce every ounce of gold and silver they could lay their hands on.

The chiefs returned some hours later with several hundred pounds of precious metal, but nowhere near the hoard that had been left behind. Furious, Cortes ordered them to produce the rest—if they knew what was good for them. The Indians stood their ground. They admitted to knowing about Montezuma's treasure, but had no idea of what had become of it. Many things had been lost forever during the siege. In any case, this was all the wealth they could find.

The soldiers began to shout and wave their weapons. Cortes, fearing a mutiny, had Cuauhtemoc and the lord of Tacuba chained like wild beasts. Oil was smeared on the soles of their feet and set on fire.

The lord of Tacuba groaned. Falling Eagle bit his lip to prevent himself from crying out. "And do you think I, then, am taking my pleasure in my bath?" he told his companion from between clenched teeth. The pirates who'd later roam the Caribbean used this same torture to find out where Spanish settlers hid their valuables. Unlike the Aztec chiefs, however, they often revealed the hiding place of their gold. Montezuma's legendary treasure was never recovered.

Whatever loot that had been collected was divided among the conquerors. After deducting the King's Fifth and Cortes's share, there was only fifty pesos left for each foot soldier and sixty pesos per cavalrymen.

The soldiers were bitter. They had fought, some of them, for thirty months almost without let-up. They had lost friends, seen terrible sights, gone hungry, and suffered wounds. Of the three hundred thousand people of Tenochtitlan, at least two hundred forty thousand had died in the siege. And for this! Why, sixty pesos couldn't buy a good secondhand crossbow.

~ ~ ~

The soldiers' misery was nothing compared to that of the Aztecs.' The end of the war hadn't brought an end to their sufferings. Tenochtitlan was uninhabitable. A day or so after the surrender, Cortes ordered the people to abandon what was left of their homes.

Under the watchful eye of his *Conquistadores*, the people trudged along the causeways, carrying their meager possessions on their backs. Soldiers, seeing pretty women, yanked them out of the crowd and set them aside to be sold as slaves. The other refugees scattered to the lakeside towns and to villages in the countryside beyond. They were not welcome. The natives remembered the glory days of the Aztec empire, days of hardship and humiliation for themselves. They greeted the refugees with curses and beatings. Some were killed, others enslaved, all robbed.

The Aztecs also remembered. In their misery they recalled the beginnings of their people, how their ancestors had wandered, despised, from place to place. Only now there was no Huitzilopochtli to point the way, or eagle to tell when they reached their destination. The proud, warlike Aztecs had lost everything in war: loved ones, property, independence. They'd lost their entire civilization.

Cortes set fire to anything in the deserted city that would burn. Standing walls, the skeletons of buildings, were torn down. The great pyramid was leveled stone by stone. Tenochtitlan disappeared beneath thirty feet of rubble mixed with human bones.

A new city rose on its ruins, the Very Noble, Notable, and Most Loyal City of Mexico. It was, and still is, a Spanish city, modeled upon those the conquerors knew and loved. The Zócalo, or Plaza of the Constitution, occupies the site

*The cathedral of Mexico City is built in part over the ruins of the
great pyramid of Tenochtitlan.*

once enclosed by the Serpent Wall. An immense cathedral
stands near the foundations of Huitzilopochtli's and Tlaloc's
pyramid. Cortes built his own palace where Montezuma's
once stood; it is gone now, replaced by the palace of the
president of the Republic of Mexico. The main avenues
follow the line of the causeways. Lake Texcoco has all but
vanished, filled in and drained during the following
centuries.

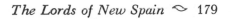

Partially cleared ruins of the Great Pyramid of Tenochtitlan as they looked in 1982. Although the temples of Huitzilopochtli and Tlaloc at the top were destroyed, the temple's steps were buried under thirty feet of earth. In the foreground at the right is a carved snake, in line with the stairway to the temple of the war god.

Yet Tenochtitlan is never far from the modern Mexican. The cypress tree where Cortes paused to weep after *La Noche Triste* still lives. Its spreading branches shade elderly couples holding hands on the benches beneath, while children play around its gnarled trunk. Within walking distance of "The Tree of the Sad Night" is a square with a plaque set in the wall. It reads: "The Place Where the Slavery Began. Here the Emperor Cuauhtemoc was made prisoner in the afternoon of 13 August 1521."

Buried beneath downtown Mexico City are entire museums full of relics waiting to be unearthed. Any building project there is bound to uncover articles from the past. These are no treasures of gold (so far), but the heritage of a people. The foundation walls of the round temple of Quetzelcoatl may be seen in the Pino Suarez subway station.

The Stone of the Sun, a huge circular calendar of stone, was dug up while excavating for a building. This twenty-four-ton calendar may be seen, together with countless other relics, in the National Museum of Anthropology in Chapultepec Park.

Mexico City came to life almost as quickly as Tenochtitlan perished. Cortes ordered the clan chiefs to bring their people for the rebuilding project. The Indians provided all the labor and construction materials. The palaces of Cortes and his captains were of red stone with massive beams of oak, cedar, and pine dragged from the mountains. The workmen, if they wanted a roof over their heads, had to build shacks in Tlatelolco or the city's outskirts; only Indian servants were allowed to live in the Spaniards' city from now on. The people were so weakened by hunger and overwork that they died by the thousands.

Few Indians benefited from the conquest. The Tlaxcalans, Cortes's firmest allies, kept their own government and were freed from taxes forever. Aztec clan chiefs were given land and control of their people, so long as they obeyed Spanish orders. Montezuma's children did very well. Cortes had promised him on his deathbed to care for the royal children. In this he kept his word. Montezuma's heirs received lands and the people to work them. Both surviving daughters became Christians and married Spanish noblemen. Their descendants still trace their roots to the Aztecs' Angry Young Lord. Nearly everyone else, however, became little more than a slave.

Cortes's captains and later Spanish settlers received large land grants to encourage them to stay in New Spain. The common soldiers were also given land in place of the gold they never received. Cortes wanted as many of his countrymen as possible in New Spain, because they would make up the army, preventing an Indian rebellion.

But, Spanish gentlemen were not supposed to work. It was considered disgraceful for a gentleman to earn a living with his hands or through trade. He might serve the king, fight in the wars or become a priest, but he didn't work. Others worked for him.

In Spain, where landlords owned thousands of acres of land, "serfs" did the farming. Serfs, from which we get the word "servant," worked for a master in return for protection and a guarantee of food and shelter. Although they usually stayed with him for life, they were not his property. He couldn't harm them or sell them. He had to let them go their own way if they met the requirements set down by the law.

But who'd do the work in New Spain? The Aztecs had no serfs, and their slaves were unlike any known in Europe. To solve the labor problem, Cortes began a system called *encomienda*, Spanish for "to give in trust." Settlers received not only land, but workers to go with it. Landowners were given entire villages, hundreds of people. They ruled these people "in trust"; that is, they protected them and taught them to be civilized in return for their labor. At least that's what they were supposed to do. Actually, the Indians were slaves, although not recognized as such by the law. They and their families were bound to the land for life. Running away was punished by torture, sometimes by the crippling loss of a leg or foot.

Many landowners were rough, cruel men who didn't care how much misery they caused as long as they had their profits. They developed a nasty custom called *aperriamento*—"dogging" the Indians. Mexicans, who'd only raised small, hairless dogs for eating, were terrified at the Spaniards' hunting dogs. Whenever a landowner made his rounds, he made sure to go with a fierce dog on a leash. God help the Indian who displeased him.

The conquered people not only suffered, they began to disappear. Smallpox, which had weakened the Aztecs before the siege of Tenochtitlan, had come to Mexico to stay. For the next three centuries smallpox epidemics broke out about every seven years. Other European diseases— measles, influenza, typhoid—took their toll, along with malaria and yellow fever, brought by slave ships from Africa. These epidemics raced through the crowded Indian communities of the Valley of Mexico. When Cortes first set eyes on Tenochtitlan in 1519, the population of the capital and the surrounding region was nearly two million; only three hundred thousand remained by 1570. The population began to grow again, slowly, during the next century, probably because the survivors began to develop immunity to the killer diseases.

Yet the pain of conquest was keener than the Mexicans' loss of health or wealth. It reached into the people's souls, leaving them unhappy and confused as never before. For thousands of years the farming peoples had thought they knew how the world worked. The forces of nature were

Aperriamento, or "dogging" the Indians. The Indians were
terrified of the Spaniards' fierce hunting dogs, which were used
to force them to work and to punish the lazy.

Sufferings of the Aztecs at the hands of the victorious Spaniards as seen by an Indian artist at the time. (Redrawn from The Misfortunes of the Conquered.*)*

ruled by gods, who might be persuaded to use them for the benefit of mankind. It was the priests' duty to teach the people how to win the gods' favor through prayer and sacrifice. Their teachings seemed to work, and the Mexicans prospered. When there was scarcity, and the people went hungry, it was because the gods were angry. But sooner or later prayers and sacrifices always set things right again, they believed.

Now the gods were gone. The *Conquistadores* had toppled their idols, burned their temples, and ended their sacrifices. Their priests were either killed or imprisoned for teaching false religion. Not only the Aztecs, but all the Mexican peoples, lived in terror. Now that the gods were overthrown, they expected the world to end any moment.

It didn't. The sun still rose in the east, moved across the sky, set, and rose again without feeding Hummingbird Wizard human blood. Clouds still clung to the mountaintops and rain fell in season without the drowning of children in honor of Tlaloc. Crops grew, winds blew, fire burned. The world continued as if the gods had never existed. But *had* they ever existed? Were they real, or the result of a people's nightmare lasting many centuries? Millions of Indians lost faith in the gods of their forefathers without (as yet) believing in the God of their conquerors.

Cortes did everything to convert them to Christianity. He never grew tired of preaching that there was only one god—his god—and that the Indians had worshipped devils. He sent to Europe for Franciscans, priests specially trained to preach and teach about Christianity. In 1524, twelve friars of the Order of St. Francis arrived in Mexico. These Franciscans belonged to an order famous for its holiness and simple living. The friars were not elaborately dressed, like the Indians' own priests; they wore tattered brown cowls, long hooded robes tied at the waist with a knotted cord. Their heads were shaven, their bodies thin from

Some of the Franciscan friars Cortes brought to New Spain to convert the Indians to Christianity, as seen by an Aztec artist.

Turning pagans into Christians. This page of Aztec picture-writing shows how the friars used symbols to make the meaning of the Christian religion clear to the Indians. The bird stands for the Holy Ghost, the figure on the cross for Christ.

fasting and hard work. Clearly these men were poor, and they walked barefoot all the way from Villa Rica.

The Indians were amazed at the Spaniards' behavior when the friars reached Mexico City. Until now the only Spaniards they'd seen were proud *Conquistadores*, who'd draw a sword or raise a whip at the slightest excuse. Yet they treated these humble priests with the greatest respect. Malinche himself knelt in the dust of the street to kiss the friars' hands and the hems of their robes. The Indians, who always went in fear of the conqueror, followed his example.

Priests flocked to New Spain during the next few years. They fanned out across the country, going to live among the Indians. They learned the native languages by bargaining with tradespeople in the marketplace or squatting in the dust to play games with the village children. They studied the Indians' way of life and their beliefs. Two priests wrote important books about the Indians of New Spain, without which we'd be ignorant about their civilization: Bernardino de Sahagún's *General History of the Things of New Spain* and Diego Durán's *History of the Indies of New Spain*. Both works have been translated into English and make fascinating reading. The friars studied the Indians not out of curiosity, but to find ways of converting them to Christianity. In time, millions of Mexicans came to the churches to be baptised and worship the strangers' God.

Once they became Christians they were not allowed to slip back into their old beliefs. They had, so to speak, passed through a gate, never to return that way. Any remnants of former beliefs were forbidden or destroyed. The Spaniards did their best to end traditional dancing and singing, because these were part of pagan belief. Anyone who sang the songs of their ancestors could be fined, whipped, and thrown in jail. Juan de Zumarraga, first bishop of Mexico, went on a rampage in the 1530s. He

A picture-map showing part of the network of churches the friars built throughout New Spain to help with the conversion of the Indians.

scoured the country, destroying five hundred temples and twenty thousand idols. Uncounted books about Indian religion, mathematics, astronomy, history, and poetry were tossed into bonfires. Zumarraga's agents did such a thorough job that fewer than two dozen books survive from preconquest Mexico. The recorded experience of centuries of Aztec civilization is lost to us forever. The Spaniards felt they were justified in destroying these records in order to save the Indians' souls.

∾   ∾   ∾

In the meantime Cortes had, or *thought* he had, all that a man could want in life. The treasures he'd sent to Spain won over King Charles, who rewarded him generously.

Cortes became governor of New Spain, captain-general of its army, and chief justice with the right to appoint government officials.

He lived like a king. Tribute that towns had once paid the Chief Speaker was now collected in his name and went into his private warehouses. Indians in one province, for example, sent him every eighty days forty-eight hundred fine cotton cloaks, plus other valuables. The largest and best tracts of land were reserved for him in Mexico City, Cuernavaca (Kwayr-na-va'-ca) and Oaxaca, where there were also rich gold mines. These lands included over a quarter-million Indians, which made him a greater lord than any in Spain except the king.

Cortes was treated like royalty. Wherever he went he was escorted by scores of servants, secretaries, butlers, chaplains, treasurers, and people to hand out gifts to the poor. An honor guard, complete with banners and trumpets, announced his arrival. The Indians, remembering their Chief Speakers, threw themselves face down on the ground as he passed. At last his dream came true. The boy from Extremadura dined in splendor, in public, to the sound of music.

Cortes lived well, but worked hard. No mere ruffian out for quick wealth, he was a builder who used his power to create a new nation, part European, part native American, out of the ruins of the Aztec empire. He hired people to teach the Indians the latest farming methods, enabling them to grow more food than they'd ever imagined. He sent to Spain and the colonies in the Caribbean for cattle, pigs, sheep, goats and chickens, none of which were native to New Spain. New plants were introduced, such as wheat, sugar cane, grapes, and peach, almond, lemon, and olive trees. Plows and other farm tools were imported, together with the craftsmen to make and repair them. Entire industries sprang up at his command. Spanish shipwrights taught Indian craftsmen how to build ocean-going vessels. Shops were set up to make nails, weave sailcloth, braid rope and boil tar, used for caulking ships. Since cannons were scarce, Cortes manufactured his own. He was so successful that he sent the king a gift of a long-barreled gun made of solid silver. He solved the gunpowder problem by sending men to dig sulphur in the crater of Popocatepetl volcano.

Under the conqueror's leadership, the peoples of the New and Old Worlds began to blend in New Spain. Soldiers, far from home, were encouraged to marry converted Indian women. Their descendants, the "mestizos," people of mixed Spanish and Indian blood, continue to play a leading role in Mexican life. Cortes also made a law against bachelors, for he wanted settlers to put down roots in the new land, not just come to get rich and return to Spain as quickly as possible. Every newcomer had to bring his wife. If he didn't have one, he had to import a woman who'd marry him at his own expense. Soon boatloads of eager señoritas were anchoring at Villa Rica.

Cortes was surprised when word came one day that *his* wife had arrived. He'd almost forgotten that he was a married man. During his stay in Cuba, he'd married Catalina Xuárez, of whom almost nothing is known. Cortes, recovering from his surprise, had her brought to Mexico City, along with her mother, a married sister, and her husband.

Catalina died childless a few months later. Her mother accused Cortes of murdering her so that he'd be free to marry a woman of the nobility. The Spanish government investigated the charge, but no crime was ever proven and we'll never know the truth. All that is certain is that Cortes, when he found her body, began to scream and hit his head against the wall.

The conqueror eventually became engaged to Doña

Juana de Zuñiga, daughter of an important noble family. The marriage, however, didn't take place until he returned to Spain several years later. Altogether Cortes had seven children who lived to adulthood. Four were born to Doña Juana, and their son, Martin, became heir to the family fortune. He also had three children with Indian women. The eldest, also named Martin, was Doña Marina's son, who became a wealthy landowner. Two other sons, one of them born to a daughter of Montezuma's, gave him much happiness in later years. Cortes seems to have been a good father, warm, loving, and generous. He was proud of his children, even though he hadn't bothered to marry all their mothers.

The conqueror needed a happy family life, for power brought neither happiness nor peace of mind. His soldiers never forgot their disappointment over the loss of Montezuma's treasure. It was rumored that Cortes had really found the treasure and kept it for himself. Each night the whitewashed walls outside his palace were scrawled with coarse soldier jokes and drawings accusing him of thievery. And each morning Cortes went out to erase them or write replies in charcoal. The graffiti finally became so annoying that he ordered it ended on penalty of harsh punishment. It stopped, but the rumors continued.

His captains, too, were resentful. Time had made them jealous of what their old commander had become. Why, they grumbled over their wine cups, should he have all the wealth, all the power, all the honor? Weren't they as good as he? He'd never have conquered New Spain without their help.

One captain's jealousy boiled over into treason. Toward the end of 1523, Cortes sent expeditions to explore and conquer lands to the south of New Spain. Alvarado invaded the area that is today Guatemala and El Salvador. He easily defeated the Indians and set up a Spanish colony;

when he died in 1541, he was buried in Guatemala City, which he had founded. His friend, Cristobal de Olid, was to take over Honduras, ruling it in Cortes's name.

Olid had other plans. Soon after arriving at his destination, he turned traitor. Honduras was a rich land, the key to the pearl fisheries of the Pacific coast of Central America. Rather than add to Cortes's wealth and glory, he declared himself an independent ruler.

Cortes became furious when he learned of Olid's treachery. It was one thing for Cortes to betray Velasquez in Cuba many years before, but it was another thing for someone to do the same to him. Worse, he knew that if Olid's revolt succeeded, others would be tempted to follow in his footsteps.

Cortes decided to punish the traitor in person. The army, which set out in October, 1524, was nothing like the force he'd first led into the Valley of Mexico. In addition to hundreds of Spanish soldiers and thousands of Indian porters, he took Doña Marina who again traveled as interpreter, and scores of private servants. Cooks and butlers saw to his food needs. Jugglers, dancers, tightrope walkers, and musicians kept him amused. He also took along Cuauhtemoc and the lord of Tacuba; he didn't trust them and wanted to keep an eye on them during his absence from Mexico City.

Instead of going to Honduras by sea, the easy way, Cortes decided to march overland. This was probably the worst decision he'd ever made. For the route lay across fifteen hundred miles of some of the worst jungle on earth. We can't be sure why he decided to go this way. He may have wanted to see the new territory with his own eyes, or perhaps let the local Indians see the conqueror and his army so they'd forget any thoughts of rebellion.

The going was easy at first. Arriving at Coatzacoalcos (Co-at-zaco-al-cos) in southern Mexico, he called the local village chiefs to a conference. Among them was the mother of Doña Marina and her stepbrother.

Mother and daughter recognized each other instantly. The old lady, remembering how she'd sold her child into slavery, began to tremble with fear. She'd done a terrible thing and expected to pay for it now with her life. Doña Marina had only to say the word and her mother and stepbrother would have been executed. But she'd learned a lot during the years of slavery and after, with the *Conquistadores*, a lot about suffering and forgiveness. Doña Marina put her arms around her mother, patted her, and soothed her with gentle words. She bore no grudges, for by selling her to the slave traders, the old lady had made it possible for her to become both a Christian and the most powerful woman in New Spain. Soon after this, she was married to Juan de Jaramillo, one of the gentlemen who'd joined the expedition for the adventure.

Little is known about Doña Marina's later life. The couple settled down on the lands Cortes gave her as a reward for her services during the conquest. There she had a daughter, also named Marina. When she died about 1540, the Indians mourned her loss as that of a true friend. Many Mexicans today, however, think of her as a traitor who helped foreigners take over their country.

Cortes's army, meanwhile, plunged into the trackless wilderness. The march to Tenochtitlan had been a spring outing, compared to the hardships they now faced. Without maps, they headed south, following compass bearings, although no one had the slightest idea where they were really going. Narrow trails wound beneath the thick tree cover. They had to cross wide rivers separated by vast swamps and quicksand bogs. Porters who took a false step were sucked under within minutes, while their companions stood by helplessly. In one hundred-mile stretch, Cortes built fifty bridges, the largest nine hundred paces long.

Each bridge was a major engineering project in which men toiled in the sweltering heat to cut, trim, and drag huge logs to the riverbanks. Unlike the march to Tenochtitlan, the local tribes gave no assistance. The villagers, frightened by the strangers' approach, set fire to their thatch huts and vanished into the jungle. Cortes's men, many of them starving, could as easily have eaten their money as used it to buy food from the natives.

These hardships changed Cortes. He became a different person. His beard showed flecks of white. His belly swelled from hunger, his eyes reddened with fever. Yet he had gone too far to turn back. Southward, always southward, he drove his ruined army.

The strain affected his judgment. When an Indian spy brought a story that Cuauhtemoc and the lord of Tacuba were planning a rebellion, he believed it without investigating further. Cuauhtemoc freely admitted that he had no love for the Spaniards. They had destroyed his city, enslaved his people, and tortured him so that his feet still ached with every step. But he was innocent of the charge against him, he said. Only a fool would plan a rebellion here, in the middle of nowhere.

Words were useless. Cortes had made up his mind that the Aztec chiefs were guilty, and they'd have to hang. Before he died, Cuauhtemoc made a speech to the assembled Spaniards. "I knew what it was, Malinche, to trust your false promises," he said. "Why do you slay me so unjustly? May God call you to account for this innocent blood!"

The executions were unpopular even with the hardboiled Spanish veterans. Bernal Diaz spoke for the men in the ranks when he wrote: "it was a most cruel and unjust sentence."

Several months later, the starving, disease-ridden army stumbled out of the jungle near Olid's settlement on the Gulf of Honduras. It was the greatest disappointment

*During the disastrous march to Honduras, Cortes's army was
often forced to build canoes to ferry its horses across rivers. The
illustration is by Gonzalo de Oviedo, from his* Natural and
General History of the Indies.

of all. Their ordeal had been for nothing. Olid was dead, executed months earlier by soldiers loyal to Cortes.

By going after the traitor in person, Cortes had, in fact, nearly destroyed everything he'd accomplished in New Spain. Letters arrived from Mexico City saying that everything was in chaos. The settlers, hearing rumors of his death, had divided into feuding groups and were fighting among themselves. One group had seized Cortes's property and executed his cousin, whom he'd left behind to care for it.

Cortes returned by sea, arriving in May, 1526, after an absence of nineteen months. The conqueror's name was like magic. Settlers and Indians turned out to welcome him with cheers and flowers. The guilty were tossed into padlocked cages to await trial.

News of these upheavals reached the royal court in Spain. Governor Velasquez, whose hatred of Cortes was lifelong, had many friends at court, and they set out to paint the conqueror as a traitor. Cortes knew about their lies and decided that he had to set things right before they did serious harm. He must return to Spain to explain his actions to the king, man to man.

～   ～   ～

Cortes arrived in Spain in the spring of 1528. Seldom has a country welcomed one of its sons with such enthusiasm. Wherever he went, he was greeted as a conquering hero who deserved the gratitude of his king and country.

During his absence Spain had become the leading power in Europe, due in part to gold shipments from the New World, which were used to pay its armies. King Charles had recently been elected Holy Roman Emperor with the title Charles V. In addition to Spain and its New World possessions, the emperor ruled Holland, Belgium, Germany, and parts of Italy.

A portrait of the King of Spain and Holy Roman Emperor Charles V was painted by the artist Titian. Although Cortes was loyal to his ruler, Charles feared that the ambitious <u>Conquistador</u> might set himself up one day as king of New Spain.

The two men met in the city of Toledo. The king-emperor waited as Cortes's procession slowly made its way up the steep hill from the plain below. The conqueror, dressed in black velvet trimmed with gold, was escorted by hundreds of soldiers in glittering armor, their pennants snapping in the breeze. In a carriage rode his aged mother, Doña Catalina, her eyes filled with tears of joy and sadness—joy at the honor shown her son, sadness that her husband hadn't lived to see this day.

Cortes and his king met for long conversations during the following days. Charles showed interest in everything about New Spain and asked probing questions. Cortes

Aztec musicians, jugglers, hunchbacks, and dwarves like these performed for the court of King Charles when Cortes returned to Spain. (Redrawn from the Codex Florentino.)

illustrated his answers with the huge collection of people
and things he'd brought along for the purpose. He showed
the royal court Aztec warriors decked in feathers and carrying sword-clubs. Onlookers marveled as Indian jugglers
and acrobats went through their acts. Some lay on their
backs, whirling balsa logs with their feet faster than the

*Birdmen. Aztec acrobats twirl around a tall pole from ropes tied
to their waists. Acrobats of this sort amazed the Spanish court
when Cortes showed them off during his visit to Charles V.*

eye could see; people gasped at the speed with which the big logs moved, not knowing that balsa is a very soft, light wood. Other performers dived from the top of a high pole, around which they spun dizzily at the end of ropes, seeming to fly. There were also bars of gold and silver, sacks full of jade, and pearls by the basket. Strange and beautiful creatures won the court's admiration: albatrosses, quetzels, armadillos, opossums, rattlesnakes, jaguars, ocelots.

Only one bit of sadness disturbed the festivities. Cortes learned that his "son," Sandoval, who had returned with him, had died in an inn. He had become so weakened from a mysterious infection that he was unable to raise his sword when the innkeeper stole gold bars from the chest next to his bed.

Charles V showed the *Conquistador* every mark of respect. He blessed his marriage to Doña Juana de Zuñiga and gave him a glorious wedding gift: a title of nobility. From now on Don Hernan Cortes would be known as the Marquis of the Valley of Oaxaca, the only *Conquistador* ever to be made a nobleman.

Once, when Cortes fell ill, Charles V visited him in his sickroom for over an hour. The royal court buzzed with excitement. No Spanish king had ever visited a subject who greeted him while flat on his back. Surely, courtiers said, that visit alone was payment for the hardships Cortes had suffered in conquering the Aztecs.

Yet one honor was refused: Charles V refused to reappoint Cortes governor of New Spain. He could be captain-general of the army. He could advise the king-emperor on any matter concerning the colonies. But he'd never again rule the country he'd conquered.

Charles V secretly feared his most famous subject. Not that he had any special reason to doubt his loyalty; indeed, the conqueror had bent over backward to prove his loyalty. But that wasn't enough. Charles V saw in Cortes an intelligent, ambitious person who knew how to get what he wanted. And some day he might want to make himself, not governor, but king of New Spain. Charles V couldn't afford to take that risk, for he needed the wealth of New Spain to pay for his wars in Europe.

Cortes returned to New Spain in 1530. His lands stretched from ocean to ocean, perhaps a quarter of the territory of Spain itself. His gold and silver mines flourished. Thousands of head of cattle bore his brand. His plantations of cotton and sugar cane showed a yearly profit. Yet he was unhappy.

Hernan Cortes wasn't made to sit behind a desk, but to do, to act—to fight and govern. But there were no more wars, and the government was in the hands of Don Antonio de Mendoza, Viceroy of New Spain. As viceroy, that is, vice-king, Mendoza's orders had the same authority as if they came from Charles V himself. A proud man, he wasn't about to let the aging conquistador meddle in affairs that weren't his concern.

Cortes fretted and became bored. To make himself feel that he was doing something worthwhile, he sent expeditions northward from the Pacific coast of New Spain. In 1532 and 1534, his ships' masters were ordered to search for a passage linking the Gulf of Mexico to the Pacific Ocean. Both expeditions ended in tragedy. All he had to show for his efforts were sunken ships, drowned sailors, and a growing stack of bills.

Cortes decided to try his luck in person in 1535. He set sail with three ships for California, which he named after a mysterious island said to exist out in the Pacific. The voyage turned out to be a replay of the disaster in Honduras. The ships were wrecked in a storm, with all supplies lost or ruined. Only one crippled vessel remained to carry the survivors home after months of hunger, thirst, and wandering.

As Viceroy of New Spain, Don Antonio de Mendoza (1490?–1552) gradually took over power from Cortes, putting the new territory directly under control of the government in Madrid.

It was a fool's errand, for until the opening of the Panama Canal in 1914, there was no all-water link between the Caribbean and Pacific. The voyage's only accomplishment was the discovery of a body of water known to North Americans as the Gulf of California and to our Latin neighbors as the Sea of Cortes.

Cortes's disagreements with Don Antonio de Mendoza seemed endless. The two men quarreled about the boundaries of Cortes's lands, among other matters, quarrels in which the viceroy always came out on top. At last, in 1540, the conqueror left for Spain with his sons, the two Martins.

The visit was a disappointment from start to finish. Special messengers invited him to the meetings of the Council of the Indies, the government department responsible for the colonies. The council members received him politely and listened to his opinions, although they never took his advice. The king-emperor, who could have settled his business in a minute, was always too busy to see the aging soldier. Cortes's day had passed. It was twenty years since the conquest of Mexico and other, younger, men were sending the riches of the New World to Spain. His own kinsman, Francisco de Pizarro, had conquered Peru in 1535, toppling the Inca empire.

Cortes joined Charles V's campaign against Algiers in 1541. For centuries Muslim pirates had used this city as a base to menace Christian shipping in the Mediterranean Sea. Their raids became so troublesome that the king-emperor vowed to end them once and for all.

He didn't. Although his army landed safely, the fleet was wrecked in a storm. Cortes escaped drowning, but lost five precious emeralds kept in a cloth bag around his neck. He'd soon lose a great deal more.

A war council was held to decide what to do next. Cortes, who had more battlefield experience than anyone around the council table, wasn't invited. He wandered about the soggy camp, bitter and muttering to himself.

When word came that the army would retreat, he flared. Retreat? Give up without even a battle? Never! That was not the way of Hernan Cortes. He offered to take Algiers if only they'd give him a few hundred Spanish and German infantrymen.

The imperial generals laughed at the idea. What would this old-timer know about fighting, *real* fighting? It was one thing to have captured Tenochtitlan, a city de-

204 ~ *Aztecs and Spaniards*

fended by ignorant savages. But, they said, Algiers was defended by soldiers as good as any in Europe. The army retreated.

The following years were miserable ones for the Marquis of the Valley of Oaxaca. Delay followed delay, postponement followed postponement of his business. Cortes, never a patient man, learned to swallow impatience with politeness and a smile.

The Spanish government's delays succeeded where hoards of Aztec warriors failed. Cortes lost confidence and gave up. "Most Catholic and Majestic King," he wrote Charles V. "For forty years I have spent my life with little sleep and bad food, my armor constantly on my back and my sword constantly at my side. I am now old, infirm, and loaded with debts. I beg you, therefore, to order the Council of the Indies to come to a decision concerning my affairs, for I am too old to wander around the world from inn to inn, but ought rather to seek my own roof in New Spain and occupy myself with the salvation of my soul, than with the fretful chores of disputed property."

No answer came to his letter, nor would one ever. For Charles V was deliberately dragging out his case. It was better, he thought, to keep Cortes wasting his time in Spain than have him bothering Don Antonio de Mendoza in Mexico City.

At last Cortes put an end to the farce. He gathered his possessions and started for Seville, intending to rent a ship to take him home. The city, bustling and prosperous, stirred old memories. He'd sailed from there for the Indies as an ambitious youth of nineteen. Now he felt his age.

While waiting for a ship, he became ill with a high fever. He couldn't eat and felt his strength draining away. The end was near, he knew, and he dictated his will. Hernan Cortes, conqueror of the Aztec empire, Marquis of the Valley of Oaxaca, died peacefully in bed on December 2, 1547, at the age of sixty-three.

∽ ∽ ∽

We'll never know what Cortes was thinking during those last moments of consciousness. Perhaps it was of past glories and companions in arms, long gone.

Or perhaps he recalled the words of an Aztec poet after the fall of Tenochtitlan, and how they also applied to him:

> There is nothing left but grief and suffering . . .
> Where once we saw beauty and valor.
> Have you grown tired of your servants?
> Are you angry with your servants,
> O Giver of life?

As he wished in his will, his bones were taken back to New Spain and buried in a church near the spot where he and Montezuma first met. No statue has ever been erected to his memory in Mexico. Modern Mexicans resent the conquest and blame him for destroying the most advanced native civilization in the New World.

Yet one fact remains. In conquering Aztec Mexico, Hernan Cortes became the founding father of that great nation that arose on its ruins.

Some More Books

Blacker, Irwin R. *Cortes and the Aztec Conquest.* New York: American Heritage Publishing Company, 1965.

Bray, Warwick. *Everyday Life of the Aztecs.* New York: G.P. Putnam's Sons, 1962.

Burland, C.A. *Montezuma: Lord of the Aztecs.* New York: G.P. Putnam's Sons, 1973.

Collis, Maurice. *Cortes and Montezuma.* New York: Harcourt, Brace & Co., 1955.

Cortes, Hernan. *Letters from Mexico.* New York: Grossman Publishers, 1971.

Crosby, Alfred, Jr. *The Columbian Exchange: Biological and Cultural Consequences of 1492.* Westport, Connecticut: Greenwood Press, 1972.

Davies, Nigel. *The Aztecs: A History.* New York: G.P. Putnam's Sons, 1974.

Diaz, Bernal, del Castillo. *The Discovery and Conquest of Mexico, 1517–1521.* New York: Farrar, Straus and Giroux, 1979.

Durán, Fray Diego. *The Aztecs: The History of the Indies of New Spain.* New York: Orion Press, 1964.

Gibson, Charles. *The Aztecs Under Spanish Rule.* Stanford, CA: Stanford University Press, 1964.

Gómara, Francisco López de. *Cortes: The Life of the Conqueror by His Secretary.* Berkeley, CA: University of California Press, 1964.

Hagen, Victor Wolfgang von. *The Ancient Sun Kingdoms of the Americas.* New York: World Publishing Company, 1960.

Johnson, William W. *Cortes.* London: Hutchinson, 1977.

Liss, Peggy K. *Mexico Under Spain, 1521–1526.* Chicago: University of Chicago Press, 1975.

Madariaga, Salvador de. *Hernan Cortes, Conqueror of Mexico.* Garden City, New York: Doubleday and Company, 1969.

Padden, R.C. *The Hummingbird and the Hawk: Conquest and Sovereignty in the Valley of Mexico, 1503–1541.* Columbus, OH: Ohio State University Press, 1967.

Peterson, Frederick A. *Ancient Mexico.* New York: G.P. Putnam's Sons, 1959.

Prescott, William H. *History of the Conquest of Mexico.* Many editions. First published in the 1860s, this book is still the most beautifully written account of the conquest. A classic.

Reed, Alma M. *The Ancient Past of Mexico.* New York: Crown Publishers, 1966.

Sahagún, Fray Bernardinao de. *Florentine Codex: General History of the Things of New Spain, Book 12, The Conquest of Mexico.* Santa Fe, NM: The School of American Research, 1955. This book contains hundreds of drawings made by Indians who lived through the conquest.

Sedgwick, Henry Dwight. *Cortes: The Conqueror.* Indianapolis: Bobbs-Merrill Company, 1926.

Soustelle, Jacques. *Daily Life of the Aztecs on the Eve of the Spanish Conquest.* Stanford, CA: Stanford University Press, 1970.

Vaillant, George C. *The Aztecs of Mexico*. Garden City, NY: Doubleday Duran, 1941. Also available in a Penguin Books paperback edition.

White, J.N.M. *Cortes and the Downfall of the Aztec Empire*. New York: St. Martin's Press, 1971.

Index

CREDITS